# DANCING WITH FIRE

## DENENE DERKSEN

# Dancing With Fire

*Two Women Who Fall Out of the Ordinary*

## Denene Derksen

First Published in Canada 2012 by Influence Publishing

Author's Photo: Anne Flanagan
Cover Design: Nicholas Jones

# Praise

*"I found the writing easy to read, and the story line was phenomenal! I loved how the two stories connected to each other, and going from one character to another, I couldn't wait to get back to the other story as soon as I started one. I also like how you threw in some education about shamanism in there. Very well done!!"*

Tina Yee, Master Stylist

*"There is much one can learn from Denene's book, much that can help us understand life's mysteries and even more importantly, much that can assist us in navigating this marvelous journey called life."*

Shanon Alexondra Harwood, Shamanic Practitioner and Master Astrologer

*"OMG!!!! That is an amazing book!!! Read the last ten pages in the almost darkness of my living room as I couldn't get up to turn a lamp on!!! Your book has spoken to many crevices inside my body and spirit..."*

Janel Ascher, Quantum Biofeedback Practitioner

This book is dedicated to Penny, and to all of the people endeavoring to dream a better world into being...

# Acknowledgements

This adventure has been made possible, and all the more pleasant, by the involvement of many wonderful people. Nicholas Jones, this book would not have been possible without your encouragement, dedication to the technical elements, and your incredible skills with graphic design. Thank you from the bottom of my heart. Thanks also to Julie and Greg Salisbury for their support and dedication to collaboration. Janel Ascher, Melissa Gent, Heather Lesley, Tina Yee, Anne Flanagan, Nancy Beaton, Mikhaila Derksen, and the other early readers for excellent feedback and enthusiasm. My Inspired Author's Circle and CAPS Fast Track group for great team energy and for teaching me to promote my work. Thanks to Michele Gunderson for opening the door to writing for me, and to the creators of NaNoWriMo for an empowering, innovative and supportive writing challenge. Karlyn Thayer and Kristen Rea at Second Draft for elevating my work to a more professional level, in a short time frame. Any mistakes in this novel are all mine! Thanks to all of my friends and family who have supported me along the way, including my grandmothers. And special thanks to my teachers, Marv and Shanon Harwood. Mucho Munay to you all.

*"What if you slept, and what if in your sleep
you dreamed, and what if in your dream
you went to heaven and there you plucked a strange
and beautiful flower, and what if when you awoke
you had the flower in your hand? Oh, what then?"*
Samuel Taylor Coleridge

*"...science will never replace sex or cotton candy."*
Gracie Hansen

# Anne 🌿

Anne took a sip of her green tea, poured oh-so-carefully from her grandmother's antique teapot, and began to cry as she noticed that she had gotten blood on the pristine white tablecloth she had set for herself. *Goddammit*, she thought. *I only brought three comfort items with me to help me feel safe, and I already wrecked one.* The urge to try to save the tablecloth was overwhelmed by the wallop of grief that burst into her controlled space, uninvited but not unexpected. She tried to contain her sobbing, but remembered she was utterly alone. If she couldn't cry now, when the hell could she? And so she let it all out. Hours of crying. When she felt the tidal pull of her grief waning, she cruelly poked into the barnacle cut that caused the stain, that caused the tears, that crumbled her sense of ok-ness. The cry of seagulls set her off again, they sound so much like mothers searching for their lost children, babies smashed into cliff walls. How could they bear to make that sound day-in, day-out? Her head felt swollen and her tea stone cold, but still she whimpered, little hiccups of pain that had been locked away for a year. *This is why I came here*, she thought, licking the blood from her hand. To bleed and cry and puke and swear, fart and masturbate and stare out to sea. *For as long as I damn well please.* The sun was beginning to set, and Anne had gotten very cold. Her cut had coagulated nicely, and still she stared, listening for help from the sea.

It had been her best friend Cecily's idea for Anne to come to the lighthouse for the winter. Cecily would never consider doing such a thing herself--too boring! But Anne was different. She always had been quiet, but for the last while she had become almost gray, in appearance and personality. How spending six months alone by the ocean was going to fix that, Cecily didn't know, but it was the only idea she had. Cecily wanted her friend back, and was willing to drive her to the coast, babysit the cat, and try this extreme experiment to perhaps bring Anne back to life. Maybe by summer they could go out dancing again.

Anne just said, "Ok. Why not?" in that flat way she had begun speaking. Prison or a resort, either was fine, everything was fine, thanks for asking. She obediently arranged a leave from her part-time job, packed a few key belongings, and watched the waves come in and out for the first week she was here, numb as usual. It was only when she got the bright idea to go right down to the dock and put her toes into the sea water that the trouble started. Goddamn shoe slipped on a goddamn slimy rock and she fell back, slicing her hand with a filthy goddamn barnacle. Sure to get horrifically infected, she would probably need to radio to get picked up and get intravenous antibiotics or something. What a joke. One week of isolation and she'd screwed it up completely already. Shit.

**Carrie**

"Daddy, you big worry-wart. It's only a week, and it's Alaska, not some booze- cruise full of horny old men. I'll be fine, fabulous even! Come on, lighten up!"

Carrie smiled at her dad with seventy-five percent of her charm. One-hundred percent would have been too much, and too obvious. She knew she was going anyways, but if her dad got too mad he might not let her use his Visa card, which would totally suck. It would be best if she left him relatively ok, for both of their sakes.

"Carrie, I just don't understand why you find it necessary to travel alone. You're only twenty-one. You think you know it all, but you don't. If you'd seen the things I've seen..." Carrie's ears closed over. She had years of practice tuning out her dad's ridiculous stories. He was a cop. Well actually he worked in the police background check office most of his career. His own experience was pretty tame, but he had collected and repeated every gory, horrifying, twisted story his pals on the force had ever told. He lived to regale her, her mom, and his drinking buddies with the most disgusting details.

"...she was twenty-five and let me tell you what they found of her would make your hair curl. You would do well to remember that," her dad finished, looking somewhat proud of himself. Carrie's mother had found Chuck's stories terrifying, and spent the last years of her life safely tucked in the kitchen, only getting groceries when her big strong pencil-pushing cop husband could take her out to the Co-op. If she ran out of something and he was drinking at the pub, she would substitute something else for the missing ingredient, creating some of the most horrific dinners known to mankind. Chuck usually had enough of a buzz on by dinner to eat a horse and like it, but Carrie stayed slim. Really slim. She took back the empties her dad thought he had stashed in the garage above the ceiling, and stocked her room with heat-and-serve food she could eat after dinner was cleared up. She ate while she did her homework, as fast as possible in order to crawl out the window sooner and play with the boys down the street. Her parents had no idea, because she was smart enough to pull off straight A's and play street hockey 'til midnight, then be safely in bed when her dad slinked in to wish her sweet dreams.

*Jesus, how could she have sweet dreams after the grotesque story he told at dinner!?* Carrie wanted to shout. But then, as now, the urge to speak her true mind was suppressed by the clever need to get her way. She bought her freedom with easy grades and charm, and even had him convinced she was going to Alaska to see the polar bears. Yeah, polar bears. As if she gave one shit about stupid, waddling bears. But she had written a report about them in grade seven, and remembered enough about them to convince her parents she had a passion for them. As if! What she did have a passion for was adventure. And possibly sex with some big burly on-the-edge-of-scary Alaskan frontier man. That was something to get excited about. Being ravaged by a tough man who was absolutely nothing like her pathetic excuse-for-a-man dad, that would rock her world, which was sorely due for a little rocking.

# Anne 🌱

Anne awoke to the sound of waves crashing against the rocks below the lighthouse…again. As usual. Little had changed here since she arrived. Even the weather seemed unusually consistent. But Anne felt different. For the first time in over a year she could breathe all the way in. It seemed she'd cried out all of the sludge that had been sitting in her chest. She enjoyed another deep breath of chilly sea air. A small smile crawled onto her face, a smile that actually had some sincerity. She relished the moment, then went to make tea. Her grandmother's teapot was cracked and yellow with age, but the beauty of the flowers, little blue forget-me-nots dancing around the edges, had never faded for Anne. She loved the teapot when she was a child, and took it from her grandmother's house during the wake, stealthily placing it in the trunk of her car when no one was looking. Anne traced her fingers along the forget-me-not's path, sipping tea and remembering bits of dreams. Her dreams had been so different since she arrived at the lighthouse. She used to dream about the baby all of the time, waking up crying and weary of life, dragging herself through another day, willing herself to forget. But this morning she was trying to remember. Mermaids, she thought, something about mermaids. Well, one mermaid. That was it, one beautiful lonely mermaid calling out to her to come down to the shore and visit with her. *Yikes, better call my shrink,* Anne thought, but she was smiling. *What a whack job I am turning out to be!*

Anne finished her tea and gazed out the window. She had a few small responsibilities to attend to, but for the most part her time was her own. With Polysporin, the barnacle cut on her hand had healed nicely, and she felt the urge to try to scramble down to the tiny beach. When the tide was low, she has the most perfect miniature beach, with a narrow overgrown path leading down to it. *Someone else has made it down there, obviously, so why can't I?* Anne pondered. As she sat and tried to shore up the courage, the clouds broke and she saw her first glimpse of sunlight in two weeks. *Well, that must be a sign. Off I go.* Congratulating herself on her common sense, Anne tied up the "sturdy practical" shoes she bought just for the trip. Grandma shoes. Maybe they would get her to the beach in one piece. Oh, and back up here, yes that too! Fueled by her new ability to breathe properly, she put on a beige windbreaker and opened the door, marching purposefully toward the path. She was not a superstitious person by nature. Sure, the sunlight shining through was nice, but she was well aware of the fact that Ernie, the lighthouse keeper's keeper, would be pulling up at her little dock this afternoon with her week's supplies. So if she did manage to dash her head against the rocks, someone would be here to clean up the mess.

*Is that the best I can do at positive thinking?* Anne wondered, shaking her head at herself. The pathway was so grown over that Anne had to trample the grass, rather than risk getting her foot tangled up underneath it. "Sorry," she muttered to the grass, as if she was doing it personal insult. The path was steeper than it looked from above, and Anne's stomach started to churn as she struggled to keep her center of gravity close to the wall. Some small part of her wondered what it would feel like to just let go, run down the path and take wing. That little voice was promptly told to shut up. It was too distracting! Anne cringed as she sliced her pinkie on the sharp edge of a dried-out bush after grabbing at it for support. She winced in pain and said sorry to the plant as she felt it dislodge from its fragile rooting in the rock face. Feeling guilty and arrogant, Anne considered turning back, but realized she was over half-way down. Stopping to breathe, she noticed a disturbance in the water, far off in the distance. *Whales?* she wondered hopefully, straining to see. Her foot slid away, and she fell flat on her butt, sliding the rest of the way down efficiently and painfully. Upon landing at the bottom, her humiliation was quickly replaced with joy. This was singularly the most serene spot she has ever experienced. Ignoring the dampness soaking into her pants, she sat and felt the friendly energy of her little cove. Yes, it was hers now. Her own piece of heaven.

*No one will ever understand this,* she thought, looking around her cove. It was nothing so special to look at, just a sandy little spot at the bottom of a rock wall. The sand was damp and flat, covered with little green bits of seaweed left behind as the tide went out, and at the water's edge there was a band of stones rolling in the waves, beautifully polished round black and white pebbles. Anne got up, brushing off her sandy bottom, and began exploring the little beach, picking up stones and putting them in her pocket. There were very few shells, but some gymnastically twisted driftwood had accumulated in a cranny on her right. She worked her way into it, pulling out pieces of driftwood and admiring their natural beauty. She envisioned taking some of them home and arranging them in her front garden, an act of creativity her grandmother would have been proud of. Just as Anne was shoving a perfectly crazy stick down the back of her pants to take it up to the top, she noticed that one of the pieces of driftwood was different than the rest. It was whiter and heavier looking. She felt an unusual chill flood her bloodstream as she extended her hand toward the stick, determined to pick it up and have a look, despite the instinctual urge she felt to run away, fast, and not look back. Her finger touched it, running softly along its edge, and she had to admit to what she really already knew. It was a bone. And it looked human. A raven shrieked above Anne's head and she grabbed the bone and scrambled back up to the lighthouse.

 Carrie

It was Carrie's second day at sea, and she was a little bored, and a little hung over. She had positioned herself up on deck, wild hair tucked into a ponytail, huge bug-like sunglasses on. She looked like she was reading, but she was strategically placed along the first mate's walk to the bridge. She had an awesome time last night, hanging around the bar 'til long after the oldsters crashed, getting to know the Polynesian bartender very well. He was a big guy, more jolly big than muscular big, and she flirted but didn't follow through with him. She had her eyes on a much more interesting catch. He was tall, lanky, and of Native Indian descent, officious and professional in his sharp white suit. He had some smolder in those dark brown eyes. As much as he tried to hide it, Carrie could tell this was a man who was connected to the earth, and to his manliness, white shiny shoes notwithstanding. She felt the heat in her belly when she imagined corrupting him out of that uniform. Which was good, the heat, because apparently no one on this type of cruise brought a bikini but her! She was trying to show off as much of her fake-and-bake tan as possible, but shit it was chilly with the wind. Time for another Bailey's and coffee. She darted her bare arm out from under the beach towel she had wrapped herself in, still showing cleavage somehow, just long enough to rifle through her giant red purse to grab the Bailey's bottle. Forget the coffee. She just took a long pull straight out of the bottle. More calories than lunch, but **so** worth it.

The hairs on her arms stood on end, but not because of the cold. Carrie licked a drop of Bailey's off of her top lip provocatively, knowing in her gut—or deeper than that—that her prey was watching. Twisting casually in her lounge chair, she tried to take a look without looking like she is looking. And there he was, standing by the door to the tall windowed room where Carrie imagined all of the important ship things took place. He had noticed her, of this she was sure. First Officer Youngblood. She had no idea what his name really was, but Carrie thought young and blood both sounded like excellent words to spend time with, hot and exciting. *I wonder if they made him cut off a long black braid for this job. Maybe he has it in his room, in his undershirt drawer.* This musing directed Carrie's thoughts to those sexy white undershirts some men wear under uniforms, not sloppy wife beaters but formfitting pure white singlets. How that would look against his dark skin was something she planned to find out. She overcame the cold enough to tug her beach towel up a little bit, exposing her perfectly manicured toes. There were a lot of old ladies on board with coral and red toes, but the dragon-blood shade of Carrie's toes stood out like a neon sign downtown, flashing "look here, look here, something fun and exciting is going on, come right in!" She moved her toes gently, hoping that he would be as transfixed by them as she was. When she looked up, he was gone. Shit. Carrie pulled the towel over her head for a nap.

Carrie was not a stupid woman. She knew many people would call her a slut, and not an ethical one either. She didn't care. She knew her shrink thought she was working through daddy issues with a string of unattainable edgy men. She didn't much care about that, either. What Carrie didn't understand was why everyone couldn't just accept that she *liked* it! Dangerous liaisons, spontaneous sexual escapades, men who were two degrees past bad boys, just into the truly dangerous realm—she simply enjoyed it. The excitement, the exhilaration of the quest and the victory, the moment she turned from predator to prey, as the door was locked and the true colors came out in the dark. Once she was alone with a man, or men for that matter, Carrie let go of control, utterly, and went where the experience took her. And it had taken her to some pretty interesting places, stories that would make her father's toes fall off, not just curl. It was the not knowing that she loved. She rubbed her thighs together and felt the heart-shaped scar that one of her particularly dark lovers decided to burn into her tender inner thigh with a cigarette. Carrie had felt the vibrations of her own scream rumbling through her core, and she felt absolutely alive. Sure it hurt like hell, especially the next morning when playtime began again, his thick thigh grinding into the raw wound. But it was worth it just to feel the intensity of the sensation. One day she would "accidentally" let her dad see it, bikini season at the lake perhaps, but not yet. For now it was just hers, and hers alone. Carrie rubbed her hand along the ridge of the scar, glowing with the memory, and suddenly felt a heavy weight dropped onto her feet.

"Wtf?" She popped her head from under the covers and saw FO Youngblood. He had brought her a blanket. Not so professional after all. There was hope!

"Thanks." Carrie smiled at a ninety percent wattage. "It was getting a bit chilly."

"Miss, it's more than chilly. You're about to turn blue. I would suggest you go inside and find a warm sweater. If you get sick, you might miss the best part of the trip."

He smiled at her, about ten percent charming.

*He is one cold fish,* Carrie thought, resolving even harder to crack his shell. Noticing the faint edge of a tattoo peeking just out of his uniform sleeve, Carrie beamed up at him.

"Can I see your tattoo?"

"No, miss, I don't have a tattoo. You must be referring to a mark on my skin I am unaware of. I'll go and deal with that now. Have a pleasant afternoon."

FYOB, as she called him now, walked away purposefully, leaving Carrie a bit flummoxed. She had never felt quite this, well, unsexy before. It was like he saw her as one of the blue-hairs that power walked around the ship every morning and evening, in their polyester pants and ugly shoes. Carrie should have been mad, but she felt intrigued, and a little odd about it. There was something about this man that was unlike anything she had ever encountered, and she planned to find out what that was.

## Anne 🌱

Anne drank her third cup of tea, still staring transfixed at the bone on her kitchen table, on the white, slightly stained tablecloth, her bloodstain now dark brown and ugly. The bone was not ugly. It was white, and dry, with beautiful long lines running along its side. It was about ten inches long, flaring out a bit at each end. There were a few bumps and grooves along its edge, and Anne could not get enough of them. She studied the bone from every possible angle, traveling up and down its length over and over again. A bone. What an absurd thing to find. She tried to imagine it as part of a whole skeleton, maybe a seal's fin? Possibly some random part of a whale? She had spent the afternoon imagining sea creatures and how this part could fit into their body, but had come up with nothing that seemed to make sense. For a moment the idea of a child's leg bone flashed into her mind, and the horror she felt was enough to make her consider throwing the bone off of the cliff, back into the sea. Of course children die, people die, all the time, but that reality lived at the edge of her mind, pushed aside a long time ago, to be dealt with some day in the distant future. Anne ran her fingertip up and down the bone, falling in love with it somehow, in a nonsensical way.

"Ha," she started, taking herself to get a tea refill, "that's the most intimate I've been with anyone in years. This is really pathetic."

Deciding to take a break from her strange obsession, Anne put on a heavy jacket and went outside for a brisk walk along the cliff's edge. The weather had not been welcoming, but Anne had not given up. Every day she walked for twenty minutes or more, to the end of a smaller spit, to look back at her lighthouse, and out to the sea, toward land, what was left of her life back on the mainland. Every day she braved the wind and the cold sea spray, putting one leather-soled foot in front of the other, taking herself to the spot closest to home. And she remembered. A little bit at a time. The time before. The sense of excitement and anticipation. The perfect house, perfect street, perfectly arranged life. Anne let herself ask some of the hard questions she had been ignoring. What the hell happened? Why did it all go so terribly wrong? Did David even love her at all, or just the life they thought they were creating? And the real kicker, what was she living for now? After a few tortuous moments, a frozen Anne, usually with icy tears running down her cheeks, walked back into the cozy kitchen to make tea and return to the art of ignoring her life.

That was, until she found the bone. Now she did her work, but strode back into the house to be with the bone again. There was just something comforting about it. Macabre and creepy, yes, but also soothing. Anne grabbed her sketchbook, an impulsive addition to her duffle bag at the last moment, and tried over and over again to capture the elegant beauty of the bone. The pencil she tried to use was not right, so she decided to create her own charcoal. After enjoying relaxing in front of a fire one night, she began to use the leftover coals to carefully smudge the gentle surface of the paper, trying to capture the bone in detail, but also to capture the perfect flow of it. This had led to more evening fires, as the result was never quite good enough.

"Why don't you tell me your story?" Anne asked the bone aloud one morning, and the ravens laughed outside. *I feel like Tom Hanks talking to his damn volleyball.* Anne feared that the isolation of the last three weeks may have pushed her over the edge, but the urge to talk to—no, to listen to the bone wouldn't go away. And her dreams, every night, were rich and convoluted. Emerald green evening dresses, shimmering scales, mermaids sunning themselves out on the rocks, inviting her to come join them. She was missing the fun. Anne was not a quitter. If she were, the darkness of some of the dreams would have had her radio for a ride home long ago. But she was stoic, riding the waves her subconscious threw at her every night, finding solace in the chalky white surface of the bone every morning. It had become her talisman, her counselor, and she was grateful for it. Occasionally Anne stood at the edge of the path down to her beach, considering risking her neck to find another piece of Serena, the name she has secretly given the bone. Serena was named for the sirens, the mythical sea creatures who could seduce sailors. But also for the serenity she found in the bone's presence. Today, for the third day in a row, Anne turned back and went inside. Her curiosity to see if there were more pieces of her puzzle down there was not strong enough yet to make the journey down. Somehow Serena was enough for now.

 Carrie

"Hmmm, how drunk would I have to be to dance the fucking Macarena?" Carrie slurred to herself, willing to use any excuse to get plastered. She was having serious second thoughts about the sexy factor on this cruise. When she saw the pictures online, it must have reminded her of the *Titanic*, and instead of seeing the wrinkly truth, she imagined a boy named Jack drawing pictures of her naked. Compared to the *Titanic*, this cruise was like a floating old folks' home. They waddled around doing whatever the schedule told them is fun, and it was driving Carrie to drink. The martini bar was moderately cool, but the disco was an embarrassing montage of every bad wedding reception she had ever suffered through. Carrie had restlessly prowled every bar on this ship, looking for fun, even a hint of it.

*There must be a crew party floor somewhere. How the hell do I get in there? The dance shows are filled with skinny bitches and flamboyant guys. They must party sometimes, but where? And how do I get in?*

FOYB had been hard to find, too. The only time she talked to him had been a rather embarrassing incident in the casino. Carrie figured she could save a little cash if she found some nice little sugar daddy to buy her drinks. Just drunk enough to look past dentures, she had talked to every single old dude in the casino, coming up with one shiny old fella who asked her to sit on his lap. She sat beside him and ordered a pair of martinis, and asked him all about his special self. At first it was fine. She kept drinking and listening, he kept drinking and talking. "Wow, a paint store in Abbotsford, how interesting. I love color," Carrie choked out, eyeing the cash in his wallet, wondering if he would need to pee and leave it lying on the bar. Well, he kind of peed, but out of his eyes! One minute the old fart was talking about paint company policies being unfair, then about how unfair life is, to have taken away his Belinda, and in such a horrible way too. Carrie sat, frozen, listening to this weepy gentleman spell out physical details of death she had not even heard from her dad. Heartbreaking accounts of neglectful doctors and his wife sitting in a pool of her own feces for a whole day while he went to the city to find a better doctor for her. The more he spoke the more upset he got, until finally he turned a mottled color and started to breathe funny. Carrie frantically waved over the bartender, who grabbed the phone in a *yeah, seen this before* manner. Within minutes who should appear but FOYB himself, in his white shiny glory. Carrie knew better than to flirt full on in a medical moment, but she did manage to catch a glimpse of his tattoo as he put his arms around the old man to lay him down on the barroom floor. *Yup, it was some kind of tattoo, maybe a jail tat. How cool.* Carrie squatted down on the floor beside him, hoping to flash her red panties his way. The high heels and the martinis made this a bad gamble, and she fell unceremoniously sideways, squashing poor Mr. Miller's hand with her knee.

"Ooohhh" he moaned, and FOYB gave Carrie a look that was not exactly smoldering. More like deeply pissed. Shit. Carrie worked her way back up to a standing position with a touch of dignity, and stood waiting for some kind of a sign from FOYB. Nothing. He just went off with the ship's medic, who took Mr. Miller to the sick bay for a good rest. "Somewhere a little safer," she heard FOYB mutter under his breath. Double shit.

## Anne

White bloated animal, settled at the bottom of the ocean. Small tendrils of flesh floating gracefully with the ocean's current. Anne felt the sandy floor beneath her belly, and primal hunger as she chopped off a finger and brought it greedily into her mouth, then tore a slice of icy flesh from along the arm of the animal, holding the next bite while still getting the finger down her throat. The arm did not bleed. The ocean already leached out all of the blood for itself. The removal of the strip of meat exposed the edge of a blue-white bone. Anne felt part Anne, part crab, as she noticed the visceral sensation of relief when the finger made it into her belly. Both fascinated and revolted, now she could gorge on the tender strip of arm. Anne could see that the remaining fingers had manicured nails with red nail polish on them, and a moon-shaped ring at the base of the thumb. The Anne/crab tore another strip of meat from the arm, and it got caught on the moon ring. Anne/crab's eyes were drawn to the shape of the bone near the base of the thumb. It looked familiar. It was the same as Serena, the bone she had been studying, stroking. The crab was still primordially hungry, but Anne pulled herself out of this dream so that she could make it to the toilet before vomiting—vomiting the dregs of the crab dinner she had prepared for herself earlier that evening to celebrate surviving her first month alone. White bits of partially digested crabmeat swirled around in the toilet bowl, dancing with odd green salad pieces, and the cold reminder of the dream arm made her throw up again, and again, 'til she was frozen to the core and completely empty.

Anne wiped her mouth on a towel and dragged herself back to bed to try to warm her bones. She had never felt so terrified in her life, without any rational reason. She glanced out the window and saw that the stars were out, their little bright dots the only comfort she had right now, blinking coldly at her. "I want to go home," Anne said over and over again, rocking herself back and forth with her knees bent up as close to her body as possible.

"I just want to go home. I want my mommy," she moaned, not even embarrassed at the childish desperation in her voice. Anne, once such a polished tax lawyer, once the most precise planner and professional dresser in her firm, mewled like a sick kitten and let snot and tears soak her pajamas and sheets, staring at the stars and praying for help. Help digesting the fact that she had befriended a human arm bone. Divine intervention to digest the fact that she had become aware of a lump of sickhurtness in her womb that she couldn't get out, no matter how much she vomited. Anne sensed an eyeball-sized, mucous-colored piece of pain she had not been able to let go of. Not since she woke up after the D and C, knowing that the baby she and David had already foolishly painted a room for was gone. Gone forever, never to return. Never to play with the educational toys hidden in the back of Anne's organized closet. Gone, but not forgotten. Instead, stored tightly in this heavy ball of junk in her body, poisoning her system so that no other babies could ever be conceived. Lying in wait for Anne to let her guard down long enough for it to rear its head and dare Anne to look at it, digest it, just try. Just try to break it down and let its toxins circulate though her bloodstream to be removed, a process that might feel like heroin withdrawal, only worse. A pocket of pus that would almost kill her if she took it on, and certainly kill her if she ignored it any longer. No doctor could scrape this out. Anne knew instinctively that this entity was something she needed to eviscerate with will and patience, agony and wishing on stars. Snot and tears, but something more, some missing thing that eluded her right now. Not the teapot, not the tablecloth, and certainly not the professionally dry-cleaned suit hanging in her closet at home, awaiting her return to the law. Something on this island, in this lighthouse, would save her. But what?

 Carrie

*Thank God I brought the condoms,* Carrie thought. This close to a spectacular orgasm, there was no way she was letting this dumb but well-hung galloot pull out. He better be in for the long haul here. She opened her legs a little wider, entreating him to keep going just a bit deeper, deeper, until he was so far up inside her she ceased to exist. Everything ceased to exist except for the spasmodic wrenching orgasm that expanded through her whole being, and had her body jerking like an epileptic.

"Jesus Christ!" Gray, or was it Grady, shouted as he came like freight train, forgetting Carrie was anything but a pleasure-giving play-toy, forcing her body up against the headboard with all of his might.

"Sweet-Jesus-Fucking-Christ." He pounded his words into her, while pounding her head into the headboard.

"Fuck!" she shouted. "Fuck, you broke my fucking neck, you retard!" Carrie tried to throw the 250-pounder off of her body with her hips and grabbed the side of her neck.

"Jesus Christ, what the fuck were you thinking? I'm fucking dying here," she shrieked, anger flooding as she felt ripped off, jerked out of the end of a miraculous orgasm by intense pain.

"Whoa, hold it, don't fuckin' die on me. I'll be in so much shit if you die!"

Pulling his dick out so fast he left the condom inside Carrie, Grayson jumped off the bed and grabbed his pants.

"Um, a little help here, you prick?" Carrie spit out. "I can't feel my fucking arm, no fucking shit here. And my neck fucking hurts. Don't you dare fuck off on me, or your boss will hear all about how you just raped me. Get me some fucking ice, right now!"

Carrie yanked the condom out of her and threw it with a violent splat against the wall. "Ow! Fuck!" she growled at herself for moving too much.

Lying naked on the bed, Carrie held her neck with her good arm, tears sneaking out of her eyes.

*This fucking fucking hurts,* she thought, saying the words over and over again as if the mantra would distract her from the pain of torn tissue. She didn't want to move, just breathed in and out through pursed lips, the sound taking her mind off of the pain. For a split second Carrie imagined that Grayson has fucked off, and would leave her alone with this pain, and the idea scared a part of her she didn't even know she had, a part of her that knew, despite her utter denial of it, that she was, indeed, mortal like the rest of them. Before she got a chance to really look at that part, the door burst open and half-naked Grayson came in with a bag of ice.

"Ice it, ice and rest. Don't move. Can you breathe?" Bits and pieces of last year's first-aid training poured out of his mouth. "I never fucked a girl to death. Fuck, this is crazy. What are we going to do?"

"Shut the fuck up would be a great place to start, asshole."

A tiny bit of fear snuck into that sentence, causing Carrie to get angrier.

"This is what we're going to do. In the black bag on my bathroom counter is a pack of Advil. Over there is what's left of the vodka. You're going to get me both, and I am going to keep taking them until it doesn't hurt anymore. And you are fucking staying here until I feel better."

Her right arm still wouldn't respond, but Carrie didn't tell the coward about that. He'd definitely take off if he realized she was paralyzed.

"Ok, here ya go. Bottoms up wench," Grayson said, with a crazed hopeful smile, as if he were some deranged fairy godmother with an attitude. As if acting tough would fix everything. As if.

Sitting up to drink the pills down almost made Carrie sick, but she managed to choke down six or seven Advils. *That oughta do it*, she thought, moving carefully back down the bed to lie down and rest 'til the pain went away.

"Cover me up, dickwad."

"Oh, yeah, sorry." Grayson awkwardly picked the bedclothes off of the floor, unceremoniously dumping them over her naked and still-smoking-hot body. He actually started to get a bit turned on, then remembered how much trouble he might be in.

"Um, do you, like, want anything else?" he asked, awkward again.

Carrie's breathing had slowed down, and it took her a minute to answer.

"Just don't fucking leave 'til I get up. It'll be fine in an hour or so. Just watch TV or something. Don't fucking leave or I'll get you thrown overboard. Just watch some stupid…" Her voice faded away as the chemical soup hit her already-exhausted sys tem. Grayson turned on the TV, and stole some snacks out of the gift basket, sitting down beside the bed.

"Nothing fucking on," he grumbled.

Anne

Tap tap tap, tap tap tap. Anne awoke to the sound of a raven trying to break open an oyster shell just outside of her window. Tap tap tap, tap tap tap. The sound stopped, and Anne pictured the bird victoriously sliding the shimmery oyster meat down its craw. Which brought it all back to her. The dream, and the thing in her abdomen. By the light of day, it seemed a little less heartbreaking, not so plausible really. But she knew she had stumbled onto something really important. Whatever it was, something in her she needed to get out, somehow. Feeling her bare feet against the rough wooden floor in a new *grateful for not being a crab* kind of way, Anne went to relieve herself in the bathroom. She was arrested by the look in her eyes. Despite all of the weirdness of this trip, she saw something in her eyes she had never seen before. A spark. A dance of black shininess, like the feathers of the ravens that surround her here. Not oily black, but a deep black that seemed to hold a universe worth of light.

As she stared into her own eyes, feeling almost hypnotized, her face slowly morphed into the face of an old woman, a severe, dark-skinned old woman who had lived a lot of life, and didn't take shit from anyone, with skin lined with deep wrinkles Anne longed to touch, to probe to see just how deep they ran. She had gray hair tied back off of her face, earlobes exposed, with stretched holes in them from some kind of earrings. Anne was captivated by this face, and the sparse dark hairs growing near The Woman's top lip. The old woman smiled at Anne, and suddenly she just felt better. About everything. Full of a wise peace that knew everything was exactly as it should be. Anne smiled back, and with a wink, the old woman was gone, and Anne's own tired-but-relieved face was looking back at her again. Anne went to her sketchbook, and spent the next three hours trying to recapture that face. The final result was far from perfect, but contained a grain of what Anne loved in the face, and she proudly stuck the picture up on the wall with a tack, so she could see it from her chair, drinking tea and reexamining Serena. The bone looked a bit severe today, like it was still cold from the ocean floor scene. Anne felt like getting rid of it, but instead just sat with it. Sat with the bone, and the old woman, and breathed. Her sense of calm slowly slid into a deep curiosity about the crevice down on the beach. If there were more bones in there, Anne needed to find them. To bring them back together. She winked up at the old woman and went to put her shoes on, tying them extra tight for gripping on the rocky path.

 Carrie

"Hey dickwad, get me a glass of water," Carrie croaked. She was only partly awake, and thirsty as hell. She tried to move her neck and found it almost solidly locked into place. Her arm was tingly, and she quickly wiggled her fingers a bit. Thank God, they were moving, all was well. Her relief was replaced with annoyance.

"Grady, you dickhead, I really need a goddamn drink of water. Where the fuck are you, anyway?"

Carrie heard the toilet flush, and the sink run. She was oddly relieved to hear that the wiener washed his hands, and then proceeded to judge him as a momma's boy for doing it for so long. Finally the door opened, and Carrie carefully twisted her whole torso to scowl at the bastard.

"Took you long enough…" she muttered, slowly realizing that this boy had lost a lot of weight in the last while. His skin has gotten darker, and, oh shit, those intelligent obsidian eyes were just not his. It was FOYB. In her room. In shorts and a blue t-shirt.

*Oh my God, I must look like shit!*

"Sit up and drink this tea," FOYB said, with a hint of annoyance. This was exactly the kind of bullshit he had to deal with on the Mexican booze cruises. Stupid rich girls and boys pissing their own pants and causing no end of trouble, financed by their parents' credit cards.

Carrie could feel his disproval, and sat up carefully, grateful for his solidity. She felt a deep need to prove him wrong, to prove to him that she was not just a stupid tart. Watching as he carefully picked up the used condom from the floor by the wall and threw it in the garbage, she realized that may take some effort.

"Why are you here?" Carrie asked in a tone she hoped was respectful.

"Oh, I'm the lucky son of a bitch the morons on this ship turn to when they get in over their heads," he answered abruptly.

Carrie took a sip of tea. It was a black bitter drink she had never tasted before. "What the fuck is….um, just what am I drinking?"

Something about his demeanor, his energy taking up every ounce of oxygen in the room, caused Carrie to speak to him in a tone of voice she never used. She could tell that he saw right through her as he stared at her with his dark brown eyes. Carrie wished he would touch her. On the arm, on the face, anywhere! Just one touch.

"That's an herbal tea my grandmother makes. You don't really want to know what's in it. Just drink it and maybe pay attention to the fact that you can move your arm now."

"Ok," Carrie said, humbly taking a sip then almost choking as it hit her. How did he know her arm wasn't moving? She hadn't even told the boy she was screwing about that. Suddenly she felt extremely uncomfortable with him in the room. She tried to sit up a little higher, wishing she could bolt.

"You've torn a little tissue in your right neck muscles, and shocked some nerves associated with your arm. They're recovering nicely now. Keep that pack on your neck and drink all of the tea. And no more vodka for awhile."

Carrie noticed just now that a weird-smelling cloth was taped loosely around her neck. It felt warm and kind of tingly against her skin, but reeked like a dirty beach. She wanted to ask what it is, but felt shy about her, well, the whole embarrassing situation!

"Can you tell me your name?" she asked.

"You can call me Mateo. That's what the guys on the ship call me."

There was an odd pause as Carrie tried to decipher the hidden message. How many names did this dude have? She studied his forearm and was transfixed by his mysterious nature. The hidden denied tattoo—was it covered by his watch? The name thing, and oh, yeah, somehow knowing what was going on in her body. Carrie flushed warmly as she realized there were other sensations going on in her body that she would prefer he did not know about right now!

Mateo helped her to finish the black gunky tea, and laid her back down on the bed. He tucked the comforter around her gently and efficiently, and Carrie thought she might have just fallen in love. No one, not even her mom, and especially not her dad, had ever treated her with such undemanding tenderness. She inhaled the spicy scent of him, and closed her eyes to memorize the moment.

"Ok, miss, I'll come back and check on you in a few hours. Please rest until then." Carrie mumbled an "umm-hmm" as she faded away into a deeper sleep than she had ever experienced.

Strong hands were massaging Carrie's calf muscles, hands big enough to go almost the entire way around her leg. Slowly and firmly the hands made their way up her legs, now changing to two hands on one thigh, massaging upward, stopping just shy of brushing against her pubic mound. So close. The hands changed to the other leg, and Carrie willed them to come just a tiny bit higher, but they didn't oblige. Instead, the hands found her heart-shaped scar, and began tenderly feeling all around its edges, inner and outer, feeling the uneven texture of the burned flesh. Carrie felt a rush of sweetness and love from those hands that she could never have imagined. The hands left the scar behind and worked their way around the sides of her hips and onto her stomach. She realized she was completely naked, but didn't care one bit. She was warm enough from the heat the hands were generating, and utterly relaxed. The hands begin to massage her stomach, going around and around slowly, sinking in deeper, in a gentle way. Her body loved this, and invited the hands to touch her deepest parts, caress her organs even. The hands moved up to her breasts, and Carrie felt a hole opening inside of her femaleness, a hole that wanted to be filled with these hands. She wanted to say something, to urge the ghost hands to reveal the rest of the body they were attached to, and for that body to come inside of her. But she felt hypnotized, unable to speak or move a muscle. Now they were working on her well-toned arms, finding all of the contours and massaging her fingers is a blissful way. When both arms were done, the hands slid under her back, and began to massage her neck. She expected to feel pain, but only felt the warm sensation intensifying, spreading deeply into her neck and making her muscles soft and pliable. The fingers on the hand probed right to the bones in her neck, and she noticed a stream of liquid heat shoot down both of her arms. *I must have died and gone to heaven*, she thought, as the hands massaged her scalp, moving the skin on her head all around in a gentle dance that had Carrie feeling as if her entire head was getting bigger somehow, expanding. She sensed that the hands were nearly finished, and wished they would start at her feet and do the entire massage again, but instead she dozed off, fading away to some faraway place.

When Carrie woke up, she was alone in her dark cabin. The poultice had slipped down a bit, and she was still tucked in tightly. Her body felt warm, hot even. Not just at the memory of the strong hands, but like fire was flowing through her blood-stream, activating her entire system. And she had to pee. Slowly she worked her way out of the bed, moving her neck in tiny little increments as she found her way to the loo. She felt no pain. Not only that, when she went to wipe herself, she remembered that not too long ago that arm was not even moving. Now it was efficiently doing the menial task it had done thousands of times. *How?* she wondered. Carrie turned on the light and looked at herself in the mirror. Oh my. She had no pain and a working arm, but she also had a giant black bruise running from the top of her neck to the top of her shoulder, darkness pooling in the cleft of her collarbone. An ugly bruise that reminded her just how much it hurt before, just how afraid she had been. And now, other than the mark, she felt one hundred percent. Well, a little fuzzy, and her breath was gross, but other than that, pretty damn good. She touched her breasts and remembered the massage she dreamed about. The best dream ever, she thought, wondering if she could just sleep and have that dream over and over again. Her hand and her eyes moved down to massage the heart-shaped scar on her inner thigh, and somehow she forgot which side it was on. That's weird, she thought, and languidly put her hand in place to rub it on her other thigh. It was not there. She pulled her thighs open and gynecologically explored herself in the mirror. Her scar was completely gone. There was not even a trace of it, not on either side. Carrie stood, transfixed, staring at her inner thighs for the longest time, wondering what on earth was happening to her. Her thoughts were interrupted by a knock on the stateroom door. *Oh my God, I hope it isn't Mateo*, she thought, followed immediately by *Oh my God, I hope it's him.*

# Anne 🜨

The stone in Anne's hand was cold when she picked it up, but now that the heat from her hand had warmed it up, it almost seemed to be glowing. When she closed her eyes, she imagined that it was sending waves of warm energy up along her arm, and into her heart. *This is a keeper*, she thought, remaining still and staring out to sea. Suddenly it was time, time to go seek more of Serena. Never mind the fear. The path was not that steep, and five weeks of no lattes has actually trimmed Anne down a bit. She felt strong and capable. The path was a little damp, so she took care, but still soldiered on down, not even stopping to pick up any more stones. Before she knew it, she was on her little beach, and the smell of the sea was both stronger and softer. The chill seeped through her brown wooly sweater, and her hands were chilled, but she made her way to the crevasse and pulled out three choice pieces of driftwood. They were waterlogged and heavy, not nearly as beautiful as the bone she had up top, and Anne left them in a pile by her feet. She reached deeper within the crevasse, into a dark mysterious place, and felt some trepidation. Her hands didn't want to go in there. It wasn't safe. Anne paused, shoving her hands down into her pockets to warm them, maybe rub some courage into them. She glanced up the cliff wall, and just above her head, lodged between a tree root and a crack in the rock, was a foreign-looking object, too white to be here. Anne piled the driftwood she already harvested against the edge, and climbed on top of the pieces, straining to reach for the bone, which had a loop at the bottom, reminding her of the mythical brass ring. She was still a foot too low, and decided to climb up the rock face. She shoved her right toe as far into a crack as she could, grabbed for a tree root above her, and pulled herself up. "Don't look down." She heard her father's voice in her head, her biggest fan before he passed. Anne found a spot for her left foot, and pulled herself a little higher, digging icy fingers into the small opening near the bone. Just a little higher. Her back screamed as she tried to get her right foot into a higher purchase, arms straining with the weight.

*This is crazy,* she thought, almost chickening out, but her hand touched the edge of the perched bone and she recognized it, knew it was a part of Serena. She willed her arm to grow longer, and her fingers wrapped around the exposed loop, tugging it out of its hiding place. It came out all at once, showering Anne with dirt, and she lost her balance. She unconsciously threw the bone to the ground as she struggled to keep from falling. It was not that far, but the rocks were razor-sharp down there, where the ocean had been slicing through them for eons. She took a breath and righted herself, then began gingerly working her way down. With two feet firmly on the sand, she gently warmed her stiff fingers, noticing where the rock edge had cut her. One of her nails was split, already turning a bit purple. Concern for the bone trumped concern for her hands, and she walked over to where it landed, poised safely on the sand. She knew immediately that it was a pelvis. The beauty of the butterfly shape captivated her. How could something so functional, so reliable, have such symmetry and grace? Anne backed out of the wind and leaned against the cliff wall, holding the pelvis tenderly, like a baby. Now her fingers had a whole new terrain to explore, holes and curves, places to weave in and out of the pelvis. Shyly she held it up against her own pelvis, one part of her brain scientifically comparing the size, almost the same, and the other part feeling an odd sensual pleasure at holding it so intimately. She lost track of time exploring the pelvis, until she noticed that the tide has begun to come it. Her time was up, and she braced herself for the climb back to the top. Relishing the thought of a cup of hot tea and time inside with her new treasure, Anne slipped her arm through the central hole of the pelvis. *Certainly no one has ever had their hand in me that way, not quite like that, anyways,* she thought. Wearing the pelvis like a designer handbag, Anne steadily made her way back to the top, down the path and into the house to put on a pot of tea. Anticipating a smaller bone, a finger or arm bone, Anne had left a small sheet of paper on the table for sketching, but now she could see that the universe of the pelvis could not be captured on a small sheet. She searched the dusty kitchen and storeroom drawers until she found a roll of masking tape. Taping four sheets together, she sipped her tea and set about placing the pelvis to be drawn. Every angle was as lovely as the next. Indecision frustrated Anne, until she realized she needs to draw them all. Every surface at every possible angle. For the rest of the day, she drew and drank tea. She posted her sketches on the wall, this one looking like a crown, this one a portal to some mysterious world. Microscopic detail here, a series of spinning drawings here. The possibilities had no end, and Anne finally called it quits well after dark, exhausted and giddy at the same time. Her fingers and arms ached, but she felt high, like a pioneer who had conquered and come to love a new territory. The foreign had become familiar, more familiar to her than any lover she had had. She collapsed into bed without even brushing her teeth, hoping she would dream about the pelvis, that it would tell her its story.

The singing of whales was slowly drowned out by the barely controlled musical moaning of a woman in serious pain. She moved from low to high tones, soft to high intensity, letting the song accompany her with the pain. The air smelled of wood smoke, an earthy smell that came from the woman herself, and the furs she was lying upon. The pain wrenched through her and she wanted to give in and scream, but strong hands supported her shoulders, tenderly stroking her and easing the edge off of the pain. She wished for more of the smoky tea that helped with the pain, but it was too late for that. The searing pain demanded her attention, along with her own voice singing every note, hoping that the whales could hear her and would bring her strength. A grey-haired woman with soft hands appeared at her feet, singing her own song, and massaging her legs. A wave of pain like a giant tsumani ripped through her body, and finally she screamed, shouted bloody murder for everyone to hear. And there was release.

Anne moaned in her sleep, and came slowly to realize she was lying in a pool of blood. Warm slimy blood all over her legs and sheets. Her period had come in the night, unexpectedly. She did the math while scrambling to the bathroom to start the clean-up process. Her periods had been weird for a while now, taking longer and longer to come. The soonest she expected to deal with this would have been…one week from now? That was bizarre. She looked down in the shower, fascinated with the swirls of blood washing down her legs, around the tub, and down the drain, hopefully to fertilize some fish or something. Fish. Whales. The dream came back to in a flash, the smell of sweat and blood, the melodious wailing. *Is that who you belong to?* Anne wondered. Did her pelvis bone send her that dream to answer her wish of getting to know her owner? Anne scanned her memory for qualities of The Woman in the dream. Strong. Determined. But not invincible, not when the pain became overwhelming. And those hands on her shoulders! Anne let warm water run on her shoulders, imagining what it would feel like to have hands like that on her body, on her skin. Oxymoron hands, simultaneously strong enough to hold most of her body weight and pain, and also infinitely gentle enough to ease the pain and fear away with their soft heat. She toweled off and put a tampon in. Her instinct was to shove it in and get on with washing the sheets, but she went slowly, gently. *How would the grey-haired woman in the dream insert a tampon?* Gently. Slowly allowing her body to get used to the idea of this foreign but so-practical object. Anne held herself gently, blushing at the pleasure she feels doing such a normal activity in such an abnormal way. She stroked her pubic hair softly, like a beloved pet. It had grown in thick and coarse without regular waxing, but today Anne found herself enjoying its texture, the way she could run her fingers down through it, then make little curls with the ends. The sound of a knock at the door jolted her out of this moment. Her weekly supply delivery!

Anne fumbled around, trying to dry herself, throw on clothes, and throw away the tampon wrapper all at the same time. This ended up taking three times as long, and as she opened the door, she heard Ernie puttering away, oblivious to the fact that she was awake and hoping for a cup of tea with Ernie for a change.

She had warned Ernie ages ago that she did not require any company, that she would prefer if her food delivery was just left on the step for her. He just nodded, probably thinking she was either crazy, or going to change her mind within a week. But today Anne had really wanted to chat! She felt so certain that her bones were the answer to some local mystery, some missing woman who had a family waiting to hear about her outcome. And Ernie would have all of the facts, of course, being the man who kept all of the islanders connected with eggs, newspapers, and the odd crab dinner. Damn.

Oh well. There was another part of Anne that was worried that she might have given away too much information if she had asked too many questions. She had no intention of giving Serena up. She wanted information only, not to have Serena taken away to some sterile forensics lab. Not yet. Anne was just getting to know her.

 Carrie

The emerald green evening dress practically tore Carrie's eyes out of her head. There was no avoiding it. The shiny sequins longed to be touched, caressed by Carrie's hands as she smoothed the tight-fitting curves over her hips. It was her dress, her treasure, and for the rest of the shopping process Carrie was just going through the motions. Going into the shop, asking to try it on, yes the one on the mannequin, sorry to be a bother, but I want it. The weight of the sequined fabric against her skin, like a seaweed wrap in the spa, but much sexier. Her eyes glowed a brighter, varying mix of greens, reflecting the color and dazzle of the dress in an intoxicating way. Carrie fluffed her red curls and smiled at herself in the mirror. This was how she was born to dress. It reminded her of her Mermaid Barbie's dress, the one she would never, ever, let her friends take off of Mermaid Barbie to try on one of theirs, not even their best one. No matter how much they begged, or offered her an endless flow of colorful glamorous options for trade. Not even when Ken demanded Mermaid Barbie take it off and show him what was underneath. The other Barbies were much easier.

Carrie slipped the dress off carefully, noticing that the sequins at the edge of the scooped neckline liked to scratch at her skin when she slid them down, leaving faint trails of red. The Visa card her dad had given her for emergencies was almost full, but the charge for the dress, along with a new pair of sheer nylons, went through without any problem. As the clerk carefully wrapped the dress, Carrie glanced around. Everything in this store was for old old ladies, women who thought anchors and navy blue shoes were acceptable. Racks of fake jewelry, covered with enough giant fake pearls to impress a blind pirate. How on earth they managed to have this dress, no, **her** dress, was nothing short of a miracle. A sign that she was on the right track, that she would find what it was she had come looking for on this trip. Carrie went directly back to her room, to hang the dress in her closet with care, not allowing it to touch any of her other clothes, studying its glittery patterns with a meditative reverence reminiscent of Tibetan monks. The phrase "Captain's Table" jumped into her mind. Wasn't it possible to get invited for a swanky high-class dinner at the captain's table? Formal dress required? Finagling an invite to such a thing became Carrie's goal for the day. It absolutely merited blackmailing the fat fucker who had tried to break her neck the other night. She scurried off to his bar to get the low-down.

ooooo

"If you think you are going to get a blow job out of me for this, you're even more brain damaged than I thought, you asshole!"

Carrie was less than impressed with Grayson's attempt to make the most of his position. He wiped the bar repeatedly with a filthy 'white' bar towel, smearing the same spilled pineapple juice back and forth.

"You almost fucking killed me, remember? I can so get you fired!"

"I got you fixed up by Mateo, actually. You look totally healthy to me. Really, really healthy, yum-yum. Way too healthy to support a story like that. Sorry, sexy."

"But," she sputtered, searching for the right motivation, one that didn't involve ever seeing his dick again, or the victorious look on his fat face.

"Look, Caaar," he said smarmily, loving every minute of having something that she wanted. "That fuckhead over there in the black banana hammock and gold tooth? The seventy-year-old with the juicy forty-something wife? He's been up my ass for three days trying to get a seat at that table. I think **he'd** probably give me a blow job if I asked, or at least lend me the trophy wife. You're just going to have to do better than that. Come on sexy, what do ya say?"

"Arrgghh, you dick!" Carrie snarled. The image of herself in that gown, sitting up at the captain's table, possibly beside Mateo, was the only reason she hadn't dumped her rumrunner on Grayson's fat head.

"Ok, fine, but only if you shower first. What time do you get off?" The double entendre made her nauseous. Fuck. "I mean finish work."

"Oooh, Carrie, I get off at 8:15. And I finish work at 8:00. I am a fast showerer." Grayson winked at her with a leer.

"Fine, fuckface, I'll see you then." Carrie downed her rumrunner, the first of a shit-ton of rum she was going to need to do this deed. And something funny happened. Her neck started to hurt like hell. Pain raced up the side of her neck, driving like a spike into the tender spot just behind her ear.

"Oh God," she said, all of the color draining out of her face. Grayson sat her down and got her a water, the ill look on her face unignorable.

*I can't do it*, she thought. Last week she could have, but now her neck was telling her, you just can't do it. Not like that. "I don't need **anything** that badly," Carrie said in a hushed voice. "Just forget about it, Grayson. And thanks for the water."

She walked slowly and carefully back to her room, the bright neon colors on the carpet making her sick to her stomach. Bed. That's all she could think of. *I need my bed.* Finally she ran the gamut, just barely avoiding a silly old man going way too fast in his wheelchair to make it in time for the bingo championship. She moaned and crawled carefully into her bed, happy to be alone.

# Anne 🌿

*Dear Anna-Banana,*

*Hi sweetie! I miss you soo much! I miss your cute little face. Ok, sure, it has been a grumpy face for a while, but I miss it all the same! I think I changed my mind about you going away, I can't stand it!!! I know we said no contact, but I think maybe it is better to have you here sad than not at all, know what I mean? So I hope it is worth it! Do you feel any better yet? At least ready to talk about that fucking David and…ok never mind. I know you really hate that topic and I kinda promised not to bring it up anymore. But jeez, I'm going bonkers here! I had no idea how much I relied on our tea dates to keep me sane. I told Ali that if he didn't help me with the kids more he was going to be on his own with them. Because I would be up there with you drinking tea and recovering from the little monsters!!!! Seriously though, I am so bored. I have been drinking too much wine, starting at dinner to make cooking less mind-numbingly dull, then kind of carrying on after the kids are in bed and I am in the tub. I can't believe I can be bored and exhausted at the same time. Fertility drugs: I will kill the man who invented them! And I have been dreaming like mad…must be the full moon. Last night I dreamed you and David came over for dinner, and the kids were arguing about broccoli or something inane, and suddenly he yelled at you for something, and you yelled back, and then you grabbed a huge knife from the table and killed him!!! Right there in my dining room, blood going all over the roast beef and the kids and the ceiling. You just went ape-shit on him, crying and cutting him with that knife. Well, I woke up cause it was too harsh to be in. And I was mad at Ali all day, just for being a man. Poor guy, he had no idea why no matter what he did that day, even taking the twins to the park for two hours like a saint, I still spit poison every time I spoke to him. Does that make any sense to you? You aren't going all "Stephen King" up there alone on me, are you? Would you tell me if you were? I just need to know, after that dream, that you are ok, that nothing bad has happened to you. You did bring up a big knife, remember? You said it was to protect you from raccoons, ha ha. Well I hope it is still packed away, and I hope you are ok. Maybe even a bit good. Hey the club is having a huge retro party in May, maybe you want to go? Dress up slutty and get hammered to old tunes? Let me know, girl, all of it. Fill me in, k? Soon. Xoxoxoxoxoxoxoxoxox, Cecily*

ooooo

Furious. Full of fury, a wild storm with an evil agenda. The furies of mythology, preternaturally raged through Anne's body. Hot cold waves of a messy torrent of pure rage. Illogical and un-called for. Anne needed to smash something. She stormed outside in stocking feet and grabbed the first thing she saw, a planter with dead old flowers in it that some overly optimistic keeper had left behind. Her back muscles did a strange twist as she lifted the ceramic pot high above her head, hurling it down against a huge rock marking the path down to the beach. Smash! Phooomph. Old dry dirt flew everywhere, getting in Anne's eyes and making her cry, angry muddy tears running down her face.

"Fucking bitch. Goddamn selfish goddamn fucking bitch. How dare she. How the fuck dare she send me that letter?"

How could that cold-hearted bitch even mention her twins

to Anne, never mind fucking complain about them. Complain about them.

"Oh, poor Cecily, working so hard with her two gorgeous, fucking matching babies, and adoring husband. What a nightmare, must be brutal. Hope she fucking kills herself. That would serve her right."

Anne picked up the shards of ceramic and threw them with all of her might off of the cliff, some landing in the ocean but a few only making it to the edge of her beach.

"Fuck!"

There was no way Anne could stand to see those pieces littering up her beach, her and Serena's spot. She hurled herself down the path, with no regard for her socks, or even her feet. With a manic, feral kind of grace, she was down in a flash, picking up the offending pieces and throwing them so hard she felt something give in her shoulder. But she kept throwing 'til they were all gone, all out of sight. And the truth hit her like a door being kicked down in her head. She'd been listening to Cecily bitch about those kids for a year. In fact, it was Anne who encouraged Cecily to vent. "Go ahead, honey, tell me all about it. Oh no, it doesn't bother me, not a bit. It's just such a different situation. I don't want you to edit what you say around me. I'm fine. Here's some more tea, just relax."

What a colossal crock of shit. What an absolute bald-faced lie. Anne stood facing the sea, hunched over with grief, hands on her knees, wondering how she could have been so stupid. She was so far from fine. A hundred fucking miles. She was furious. And not even with Cecily. With God. With herself. For not doing better. For not being able to do the most simple goddamn thing her body was born to do. Why the fuck did she have all those bloody female organs for all of those years, puberty, pads, ruined panties, the fear of embarrassing odors, ill-fitting bras, even a little pot belly, why the fuck did she even have to bear all of that garbage if she couldn't even bring one little baby into this world? Not two, not twins, not eight and a TV career. Just one. Her legs gave out and she landed carelessly on the wet sand. Why was she such a fuck-up, such a waste of biological matter? The veneer of the straight-A student, the talented and successful lawyer, the woman who could miscarry on Tuesday and try to go back to work the following week, was shattered like the pot, lying in pieces all around her.

Shivering, through swollen eyes, Anne watched the impersonal ocean waves crash onto the beach, and roll back out. Smash onto the beach, and roll back out.

*Who fucking cares about me?* Anne thought. The waves just continued to do their thing, regardless of Anne and her drama. Endlessly. And slowly Anne emulated the feeling of those waves, sinking down into herself, feeling the storm of self hatred fade away. Only to be replaced with a slightly bitter aftertaste of apathy. Why bother to do anything at all? If the one time she really cared about something, really, really wanted it in her true heart of hearts, God or her body or whoever just randomly decided "ha-ha, joke's on you, you can't actually have this after all. Just kidding. Not for you, just all your friends. Cecily can even have two. But not you. How foolish of you to even imagine it could turn out."

Anne waited and listened, secretly hoping for some kind of a sign, some magical moment to tell her she was wrong, she didn't really want it that bad, she was deluded about the baby, and actually glad it didn't happen. But nothing happened. No ravens came and talked to her. No mermaids popped their shining red heads out of the water to offer her tea and sympathy. The sun didn't even manage to shine. Not one little bit.

Anne thought about her own mother, a slovenly woman who had never really liked Anne. Loved her, did the bare minimum amount of parenting someone in her social group could get away with, but there was no joy, no real connection. Shopping for Mother's Day cards was a joke, the gushing mushy cards so far from the truth that Anne always ended up buying "blank inside" cards and scribbling some sanitized generic wishes for a nice day. She wondered why she even bothered, but dutifully bought the stamp and mailed the card, every year like clockwork. Anne suddenly realized that she had felt excited about motherhood. Actually inspired by the idea that with very little effort at all she could out-do her mother's lackadaisical approach. With her grade-A effort she would be an amazing mom. A super mom who would create the most beautiful intelligent and socially adjusted child the world had ever seen. And enjoy doing it. Another balloon burst for Anne, another crock of shit revealed. Anne was obviously just as, if not more, fucked up as her mom, as Cecily, as the rest of them. Her child would be a brat, probably rebel from Anne's picture-perfect, library-research-based parenting and do a school shooting in grade six or something. Just to show Anne what a judgmental bitch she was. It was a cosmic joke and Anne was finally beginning to get the punch line.

Anne was **not** perfect, and she did **not** have control. Did not have life in a tidy package like she had spent so much energy trying to convince everyone that she did. She was, actually, living alone, getting hairy, and talking to and stroking bones, for Christ's sake. What more proof did she need? She was a total mess. Just like everybody else. And that was fucking hilarious. Anne rolled around on the cold sand, ruining her shirt, scraping her elbows, and laughing at herself. Laughing at her insanity, the never-ending cycle of waves that she couldn't change if she tried, and at what a gigantic fucking relief it was to realize she had just as much right as everyone else to be a complete loser! Suddenly eligible for Lettermans' stupid human tricks. "Arf arf, I am Anne, the barking mad seal. Watch me eat this seaweed, yum-yum."

Anne stuck her tongue out and gobbled down a filthy piece of seaweed.

"Nutritious and delicious!"

She was giddy now. She did front rolls and cartwheels on her tiny beach, feeling the sting of blood returning to her half-frozen toes and fingers. Her cheeks were burning and her heart was pumping and she felt very much alive. Dirty and ridiculous, but alive, every single cell suddenly appreciated and free to do its own little cell thing, right, wrong, or indifferent. However they wanted. She let her belly stick out, and thumped on it with mad glee.

"Oooh ooooh oooh, me so sexy, me love you looong time."

Parading across the beach, doing a burlesque show for herself, Anne became her crazy, fucked-up self, and even if someone had been watching she would not have stopped. Something in her had broken free, the dam had burst. The fish tank had shattered and the goldfish were flipping all over the countertop.

Not putting those crazy buggers back in! Look at them go!

Anne dried her long blonde hair briskly, working hard to get herself as warm as possible. The archaic hot water tank in the cottage was no match for how cold and dirty Anne was when she jumped in the shower, but she did her best. The wine Cecily sent was helping immensely! Anne had not planned on bringing any alcohol to this retreat. It seemed somehow risky, or at least counter-productive. But this new Anne thought drinking a bottle of red was a fabulous idea. If she wanted to, she could even dip into the dusty half bottle of rum she had found under the sink when she first arrived. Really, in the grand scheme of things, what difference did it make what Anne did? She took a long slug of wine to seal the plan, and put on the warmest flannel PJs she had brought. She heated up a tin of soup on the stove, leaning dangerously close to the flame to get warmed up even more. As the soup cooked, she arranged the fruit Cecily had sent her. She had no bowl big enough to be a fruit bowl. This much fruit at once was probably a first for a light-keeper. Before she knew what she was up to, she had arranged all of the fruit inside the pelvis, and placed it with a flourish on the kitchen table. It looked beautiful to her, all that lively colourful fruit embraced by the sun-baked pelvis. Anne sketched the pelvic fruit bowl as she sipped on her soup and wine. Perhaps she would feel differently in the morning, but it seemed to her that her drawing was about 100 times better than it was before. The fruit seemed to glow in the unique bowl, especially when she used the old broken crayons she found in the catch-all drawer. It was hard to imagine a child here, such a small stark living space. Perhaps it was just a visitor, a special trip out to see grandpa or something, the crayons used up and left behind. Anne posted her latest creation on the wall, then slipped into bed to cozy up and digest her soup. There was sand in her bed. How it got there was a mystery. The old Anne would have leapt out of bed, like the princess with the pea problem, and shaken the covers 'til every grain was out, then swept the floor to make sure it didn't get back in. This new Anne, however, glanced over at the unwashed dishes on the sideboard and grinned. What a slob. Whatever. She just squirmed around until the sand was mostly pushed down to the bottom, then fell into a deep sleep, the effects of the day and the wine catching up to her. She giggled to hear herself snoring a bit. She had hated when David snored, especially after a beer or six. But tonight she found snoring to be a hilarious phenomenon.

ooooo

Dreaming about having sex with David was just as disappointing as the real thing had been. Anne's subconscious still didn't find him very appealing, and the phrase 'duty sex' came to mind more often than anything else. Anne couldn't fake it. Her only lying skills were in defense of her clients. Otherwise she was annoyingly honest, and wished she could have faked something for David's sake. In the dream he rubbed his cold, untrimmed toes against her leg, reminding her of a homeless person's desperate dog trying to get a scrap of food. "Please?" the scratchy feet seemed to say. Anne stifled a shudder, and pretended to be asleep.

But David was persistent and soon they were having intercourse. That was really the best way to describe the wooden, predictable act they were performing. After David finished and fell asleep, Anne would always end up in the kitchen eating from her secret stash of Oreos, unable to sleep and wondering what Freud would do with her. *Diagnosis? Oral Oreo stimulation addiction. Needs intense counseling, maybe shock therapy.*

Sometimes Anne fantasized about being raped by some sexy therapist while she lay vulnerable on his chaise lounge. In the fantasy, there were no Oreos. Dozing into another fantasy, she turned herself into some strange, highly sexual creature and went down on David in the kitchen. She was even a little turned on as she made him come in five minutes flat. Then she stood up, wearing some sexy lingerie she never owned, and declared, "That's it. David. Hope it was good 'cause we are all done here."

She grabbed her purse and strutted out of the house in stiletto heels, which she also had never owned. She stole the keys to his Lamborghini (in real life, he drove a Neon), laughed maniacally, and tore off down the street into the sunset. Off to find a man who could make her scream, lose control, confident he was just around the corner. She took the corner too fast, and flew off of the edge, her stomach lurching as the car fell and fell.

Anne woke up just before the car hit the ground. She was scared, relieved, and still turned on.

ooooo

Cecily had also sent a vibrator. With extra batteries. When

Anne opened it, her first thought was *I hope Ernie didn't see this!* and her second one was *extra batteries, are you kidding me?* This was not the kind of thing she had the nerve to buy for herself, though Cecily was constantly urging her to try it—to take responsibility for her own sexual satisfaction, especially since David and his sporadic oral sex was long gone. The good thing about only coming every few months was that she had to do less pretending to be with someone else before she could get off and get to sleep. Anne rummaged through her drawer and grabbed the thing. It was actually kind of cute, pink and not too big. Anne could totally imagine Cecily buying some twelve-inch black wonderstick just to get a rise out of her. But this little thing seemed innocuous enough to try out. Anne lay awkwardly on the bed, holding the buzzing phallus against herself. At first there was no way anything was going to work. Even miles from home, with no human contact for weeks, Anne felt like someone was watching her. The idea of sticking a piece of plastic, a kitchen appliance's little sister, up inside herself, was nothing short of absurd. She closed her eyes and turned the intensity down a bit, and just willed herself to breathe, and relax. Don't try to make anything happen, just be with this experience. It was starting to feel a bit good, but she was also dozing off here and there. She ran through all of her old reliable fantasies, the images of past boyfriends, and front seats of cars with strangers that had worked for her in the past, but she just couldn't hold the thought long enough.

Then a man came to her in a dream. He was young, and full of confidence. His hands were rough from hard work, and his arms strong.

"Marcello," she said, kissing him and running her hands through his dark wavy hair.

"Anne, my darling," he answered. They kissed passionately, the scent of him filling Anne's heart with joy. His cheeks were rough with stubble, and grazed her face, leaving her feeling tingly and raw. His hands reached around and touched her breasts, holding each as if it were a treasure he had lost, then found again. Anne left the scene immediately when the vibrator fell down between her legs. She was partially awake, and tried her hardest to get back into the dream. She could still smell his scent, like wood smoke, spice, and fresh air rolled into one unbelievable aroma. She tried to remember the chocolate-brown eyes, and the way they looked at her with so much love, but the dream faded away, and she was left with a running vibrator in her hands, and the memory of being knee-bucklingly aroused, just by kissing.

The vibrator found its places and Anne learned how to give herself orgasms that shook her whole body. She even let herself make some noise, purring like a kitten as she ran the wet tool up and down her body, back and forth across her breasts, along the side of her neck. She lost track of time and explored until the sun began to sneak through the window. Feeling tired and exhilarated, Anne got dressed and went outside to watch her first sunrise. The pink and orange sky made her hands look pink and she felt soft. Soft and full of grace, somehow. She crawled back under her covers and fell into a satisfied sleep.

ooooo

*Dearest Cecily,*
*Well first off I want to apologize for what a bitch I have been.*

*Not out loud, no, but in my head I have been thinking the most terrible judgmental things about you. When I told you back in July that I was ok about the miscarriage and everything else, well I was just lying. Even when we found out David killed himself, despite how I felt about his going berserk, it was a shocking loss. But I felt like ice inside. When I said it was ok for you to talk about the twins, that I could handle it, that was a lie too. I couldn't admit to you that I was, no, still am heartbroken about the baby and what David did, and that the very idea that you could have two babies and Ali, and still complain, has been grinding against me this whole time. Which is totally unfair, I know. You have been a great mom and still a hot wife, and worked part time to top it off, it has been a lot for you to juggle. Especially with your best friend turning into some kind of zombie. Sending me here was a terrific idea, though you might think I'm more crazy when I tell you about some of it! Sending wine was an even better idea, more would be great! Also I need a favor. Could you go online and search to see if anyone has gone missing in this area, or near here in the last five years or so? I'll explain later, it's nothing to worry about, just something I am curious about. If you get a chance I would also love a paint set, any kind you have lying around will do. See, I am expanding my horizons! The sunsets and sunrises are beautiful here, especially with the lighthouse in the foreground, I thought it would be fun to try to paint them. Ok that is all for now, except lots and lots and lots of love to you, the boys, and Ali. You are all lucky to have each other, and I am lucky to have a friend like you. Thanks again. Ps do we know anyone named Marcello? I had the sexiest dream ever last night, and he seemed extraordinarily familiar! With love and gratitude, Anne.*

Carrie

*Dear Ms. Kearns,*

*I has come to my attention that you are traveling unaccompanied, and I was wondering if you were free for dinner tonight? Some friends and I are celebrating an anniversary of sorts, in a private dinner room on the Tango deck. We are all dressing formally. If you did not bring formal attire, I am sure they would have something for you in one of the shops. Gifts are not required. It is not that sort of anniversary. What we do require is the company of a refreshing young woman such as yourself, so I do hope that you will make yourself available. Sincerely, Mrs. Alethea Porteous.*

*What the hell?* Carrie thought. Was this the closest she was going to come to the Captain's Table, or the secret staff party? A bunch of old bats dressing up in ridiculous clothes and celebrating the anniversary of the orchid, or the invention of cricket or something stupid like that? What a horrible way to spend the evening! Even alone in the room, Carrie could think of twenty-five things to do that would be less excruciating than the granny parade. And there just had to be some good-looking men hiding on this damn ship somewhere. Carrie turned to throw the crumpled invitation into the trash can and zing, there went her neck again. "Bloody hell!" Carrie growled, afraid to move a muscle. She held the letter in her hand and waited for the spasm to pass. Waiting, waiting, swaying a little on her feet, a caged tiger preparing for a pounce. Then boom, she saw it. Written on the outside of the envelope was the name of the exclusive group she had been about to snub.

"The Scarlet Letter Society." Carrie did not remember exactly, but didn't scarlet letters have to do with hookers or something? Her tongue went across the front of her teeth, something she did every time she had a flashback to junior high, when she had a flat chest and braces. Yup, the braces were definitely gone, and she knew her knockers were phenomenal. Her dad had the surgeon's invoice to prove it. In grade eight, a very awkward group of Carrie's friends had started the "best ass" club. They weren't talking about their own asses. That would have required too much courage. The gaggle of girls would meet every Friday lunch and talk about the way guys looked in their jeans, especially the "guy with the great ass" who was at roller skating the night before. They would bring in record cover art, and compare the finer points of what made a guy's ass nice, and which rock star looked the best. Carrie felt a little nostalgia for the innocent times. By the end of grade nine, the same girls were divided into three cliques, and in fierce competition for the hottest guys. Their conversations became guarded and strategic, no one wanting to risk letting anyone know her insecurities. Carrie had tons of friends, of course, but not one of them seemed as fun or open as those silly grade eight girls on the floor outside the home ec doors. Too bad. Maybe these 'Scarlet Letter' women were actually fun? Carrie decided to go to the dinner. She would take advantage of the opportunity to wear the dress and make it count. Forgetting all about her neck, which had settled down mysteriously, Carrie went to plug in her curlers.

"Fuck 'shaft,' Leah. If I hear that word on more time, I'm going to vomit. There's got to be something better. Come on, put some effort into this!"

Carrie shook her head a little. Did she really just hear that? She was standing outside the door to the private dining suite, dressed to the nines and a little drunk. It took half a bottle of wine to get dressed, then two martinis as 'boredom insurance'. The waiter who had inspected her invitation and led her down to this door was acting really strange, like he thought she was gorgeous and terrifying at the same time. Carrie had quickly read the newspaper at the bar, trying to catch up on world politics so she didn't feel dumb or left out of the old ladies' conversation. 'Fuck shaft' was not something she had expected to hear tonight! *Hmm, what have I gotten myself into?* she wondered, knocking brightly on the door.

"Oh, do come on in, Carrie," a throaty voice barked through the door.

*That must be Alethea,* Carrie thought, and felt a shiver of fear run up her spine. That voice had balls. It carried a mega-dose of authority and a hint of something dangerous. A dragon lady voice. Carrie let herself in and was overwhelmed with a cloud of cigarette and cigar smoke. There was a strict policy of no smoking indoors, anywhere on this ship, with signs everywhere to remind you about it. How was it that these women got away with this? Maybe they are rich and powerful. Carrie put on her ninety-five percent charm smile and took a confident step though the smoky veil into the room. The table was long and laid out with glittering crystal and rich purple linens. Four women were over at a bar against the wall, dressed in an array of finery, one in bright yellow, another in a linen shift dress that was pure style. All of the women had their hair in complex up-dos that must have taken hours in the salon to complete. They stared at Carrie with glittering eyes, champagne flutes in their gloved hands, diamonds spilling here and there. One even sported a cigarette holder, and took a deep, sexual drag before crooning, "See what I told you, girls? She's absolutely fucking gorgeous. This will be an excellent evening."

Carrie stood dumbstruck as the voice carried on.

"I am Alethea, and we are the Scarlet Letter girls. We are very pleased that you have chosen to join us, and we sincerely hope that this proves to be an evening to remember for you."

Carrie stood staring, as one by one the ladies introduced themselves.

"Welcome to the dinner, Carrie. I am Ronnie, but tonight I think I will be Carmen. So call me Carmen."

Carmen was dressed in a bright yellow sundress, short enough to show legs that were surprisingly fit for her age, which was hard to peg exactly, but definitely well past grandmother. Her feet were wrapped in espadrille sandals with yellow ribbons criss-crossing up around her ankles. Carrie had to admit it, this was one energetic and sexy grandma lady!

"And I'm Leah. You may call me Leah. That will be more than acceptable for tonight for me."

Leah was the one in the linen shift dress. Carrie loved her style. It was simple and elegant at the same time. Her frame was long and slim, and her eye makeup was a little heavy, reminiscent of Cleopatra. She had copper bracelets that jingled gently when she shook Carrie's hand. Her grip was soft, but also no nonsense.

Her skin was dark brown, and Carrie had an urge to run her hand up and down the outside of Leah's arm, certain it would be warm and soft, like polished mahogany. Perhaps two martinis had been poor judgment.

"And finally, this is our Rose."

Pulling her eyes away from Leah's gold glitter eye shadow, Carrie's gaze was drawn downward to a woman in a wheelchair she had not noticed originally. She had silver-gray hair sprayed into submission into a sharp beehive. Her face was powdery and lined, with a bright tropical orange lipstick that matched her dress. Her dress glowed like an orange life raft, and was so full that the wheelchair was almost consumed by its folds. It had a low cut and long sleeves, the kind that dip down when you lift your arms up. Carrie teetered a bit on her heels as she leaned forward to shake Rose's hand, terrified she would lose her balance and hurt the tender flower of a woman. Rose grabbed Carrie's hand and yanked it forward with shocking strength. She kept pulling until Carrie fell right into her lap.

"Gotcha, girlie!" Rose shouted with glee, her eyes sparkling with mischief as she took in a deep inhalation of Carrie's hair.

" Hmm, almond scented, not too bad. I'm more of a tangerine girl myself, as you can see by my dress and shoes. Almond smell is too much like cyanide for me. Up you go then."

Carrie righted herself and hiccupped, something she only did when she was completely off balance, and this crazy old broad had thrown Carrie for quite a loop. Maybe four martinis would have been a good idea.

"What are you drinking tonight, my dear?" Alethea asked.

"Martini, if you have one?" Carrie manageed to answer, between girlish hiccups.

"I love that your name is Carrie, like on 'Sex in the City.' Are you anything like her?" Rose asked, her childish voice no match for the rascal trick she played earlier.

"Um, no, ma'am, I don't think I'm too much like her. I don't write and I don't have a group of friends like that."

"But you love men like she does, right? Or are you more of a Samantha type?" Rose cackled.

"Rose, she is clearly more of a Samantha. Put on your glasses if you can't see the tits on her. Those are not museum grade. They are definitely hands on, high-test tits!" Carmen exclaimed to Rose, with the same trucker tone as the shaft comment Carrie had overheard at the door.

"Never mind her tits, she called you ma'am! That's hilarious! Even at ninety you are more of a madame than a ma'am, and you know it, you dirty slut!" Leah threw her entire glass of champagne down her throat to punctuate her point.

"I am a dirty old whore, aren't I! And of course I know she has a fabulous set of breasts. They felt just lovely against me when she fell. They almost feel real. It's amazing what they can do nowadays."

*I think I am in the Twilight Zone,* Carrie thought, throwing a good portion of her martini into her own gullet.

"Ladies," Alethea said regally, looking like the queen of swords in her silver evening gown. "Carrie has not yet had a chance to get properly acquainted with our little group. Perhaps you would consider toning it down for a few moments?"

"Fine, mother." Rose sighed dramatically.

The others nodded. Alethea was clearly the leader of this odd bunch.

"Please, let us sit down and get ready for the first course. Perhaps Carrie would like to help us with our little game?"

The ladies refilled their drinks and made their way to the table, Leah pushing Rose's wheelchair up to an empty spot on the opposite side of the table. Each place setting was beautiful, the silver and crystal reflecting the deep eggplant and candlelight.

"The challenge, Carrie, is simple yet vexing. We're trying to create a new word to use when one wants to say penis, but not sound like a biology teacher. Leah had expressed a penchant for the word 'shaft', which unfortunately all of us have overused."

"I still like dick," Carmen said, eyes shining with admiration for her double entendre.

"Dick is quick and dirty, gets the job done."

"But Carmen," Leah said in her velvet voice, "the whole point of the game was to make up something new, uncover some edgy word we can all incorporate."

"You don't even have sex, you boring old cunny." Rose clearly tried to get the heat back into the conversation.

"Well, I don't right now, but I'm thinking about it. I want to make my murders a little more racy. But the language just annoys me so I throw it away. I just can't use pussy the way you can." Rather than being annoyed, Leah seemed to admire Rose's foul comment.

"What about you, Ginger, what words do you moan out of that sweet little mouth of yours when your man is giving it to you?"

During a pause in the banter, Carrie tried to figure out who Ginger was.

"Carmen is addressing you, Carrie darling. She finds it helpful for her juices if she randomly assigns us with sexier names."

"Umm, I, ahh, I..." Carrie floundered for words while she calculated how long it would take her to get to the door in high heels. Obviously she had managed to land smack in the middle of a coven of hideous witches.

*Oh God, the cyanide comment! And the look of fear on the waiter's face. It all makes sense! If I stay here, they will end up boiling my bones for breakfast!*

Carrie's mind raced through all of that, looking to the door and seeing it open. Thank God, she could make it now.

"I, um, I think I forgot something in my room you would really love to see..." Carrie said, getting to her feet, heart racing.

"Oh sit down, you silly goose," Alethea said with steel in her voice. "You are the only thing we want. There's nothing in your room we could possibly be interested in. And the appetizers have arrived."

Just then the waiter pushed an overloaded trolley into the room, and began to pour them all white wine as Carrie sat back down obediently. She would leave after the first course, she decided.

Elegant small plates of scallops were placed in front of each of the women, who oohed and ahhed over the beautiful plating, each with an artful drizzle of teriyaki sauce and a browned sprig of rosemary sticking up from each perfect scallop.

"Wow, Gaston, the rosemary is standing tall and firm, now isn't it. Kind of reminds you of your dick first thing in the morning, doesn't it?"

The waiter blushed a deep red and seemed to have stopped breathing. He locked eyes with Carrie, silently pleading for her to make this tangerine organza wheelchair woman stop saying things like this to him. Carrie stared back, and noticed that he was actually kind of hot. The whole atmosphere in the room was thick with tension, awkward and sexual. Then all of the Scarlet Letters broke into peals of laughter that Carrie and the waiter couldn't help but join in on. It had shifted from scary to just bizarre now that Carrie had an ally, someone who would be a witness if these birds ate her alive.

"All right, young lady. You have passed the test, we will put you out of your misery now," Alethea stated, with a warm smile on her face.

*Put me out of my misery? Is this it for me then?*

Carrie felt like her life should be passing before her eyes, but all she could think was that that waiter was pretty hot, and his dick probably merited closer examination. *How sad if I don't get the chance.* Five sets of eyes looked back and forth at each other as Alethea dragged the moment on for as long as possible. Finally Alethea let her cat out of the bag.

"We're writers, dear. Soft porn, erotica mainly. Except for Leah. She has a mind that writes the most complex murder mysteries on the market, but she loves the dick too!"

They all broke into laughter again as they watched Carrie put the pieces together, the game, the cyanide, the shaft. The hard 'c' word even, though part of her couldn't really accept that these beautifully wrinkled women could talk like this, never mind write it.

"Hey, don't forget about my phone sex job," Rose contributed proudly.

"Oh yes, Rose has found a delightful sideline for herself, talking men and women through some delicious sexual encounters on the phone. As you can hear from her voice, most of them think she is an innocent young runaway, debasing herself for money for acting classes. If they knew she was a ninety year old whore in a wheelchair, well that might slow business down a bit, but it would be fun to watch them find out!"

They all giggled and drank more wine, wiping the last of the rich sauce off of their plates with fingers or tongues.

Alethea continued. "Every year we take a trip together, looking for inspiration. And working on our dirty vocabulary as well. We do not often invite anyone to join us. I hope you consider yourself lucky to be here. You might just learn something new. And we're all hoping that you will regale us with some of your conquests. It's obvious that you are not on this cruise to work on your needlepoint."

" I'm going to need a lot more wine," Carrie said with a smile, settling back into her chair with a confident air.

ooooo

'Scrape, scrape, scrape.'

The sound of Carrie scraping her spoon against the edge of her cut crystal dessert bowl was maddening. No one was talking, and the ladies were staring at her with expectation. Carrie was stalling, and they all knew it. She couldn't believe how quickly she went from excited to defeated. Cockiness to insecurity. When her friends listened to her tales of sexploits, they would always oooh and ahh, saying "Oh my **God**" and "that must have been **amazing**" or "weren't you **scared**?"

These women were underwhelmed, to say the least. Carrie had

begun with some tamer episodes, like simultaneously jacking off two boys under a blanket on the couch at the same time, watching TV in her parents' basement. Their response had been polite at best. At first Carrie thought maybe the ladies were not as racy as they pretended to be, so she kept her stories fairly vanilla, not wanting to offend them and miss out on a delicious dinner with free wine. After the third story tanked, Carrie realized, with utter horror, that she was boring them!

Sex was the only thing she was good at, and they were bored! She bit her lip and tried to remember something that would get their attention. When she told one of her favorites about fucking the hot bartender in the parking lot, one of them actually yawned! When she dug out the time she had instigated a group-sex marathon on her boyfriend's mother's bed, one of them said, " That's so 1974!"

They enjoyed the story about the cigarette burn a bit, but were demanding that she show it to them, which she couldn't since it had disappeared! Leah was always polite, but Rose kept saying things like, "And then did he do you up the ass?" which he had not, so she was disappointed. Carmen was all about locations, and asked her a litany of "Have you ever done it in a_____" questions, some of which actually made Carrie blush a bit. But the worst was Alethea's reaction. She had listened quietly all evening, ever the polite audience. But when Carrie told the story of Grayson fucking her so hard she hurt her neck, Alethea actually interrupted her and said, "have you ever had sex with an **adult**, Carrie?"

Which is what led to this painful moment of chocolate mousse-bowl scraping. Carrie had to admit to herself that she had been playing with little boys all of her life. Stupid little games with childish men, no matter what their real age was. She had not, ever, hooked up with a man who was an adult. She was not really even sure what the difference was, but something in Alethea's tone sent the message clearly home that Carrie had, despite breaking some rules and taboos, missed the boat. She had played it safe in a way, and missed out on a real experience somehow, and that realization was depressing.

"Look, Carrie, don't be upset. I didn't intend to hurt your feelings. In fact I commend your ability to explore, and your kindness in sharing these adventures with us. Really, thank you. It's just that I'm personally trying to write at a whole new level, one that will appeal to intelligent grown women, and many of them are looking for the same thing: a man who can ravage them, fuck them up the ass, and make them a gourmet breakfast with intelligent conversation. A man who can let her rage and howl when she is upset and not take any of it personally, just listen then throw her on the bed and make her forget all about it in five minutes. A man who can take her somewhere she has never gone before, who has explored sex in many different cultures and has made up his own raw-yet-sensitive style. Those women are my readers, and they just don't get excited by the dick in pussy, juice flowing down side of leg kind of gynecological reality show anymore. They've done the experimentation themselves, and are not inspired by cliché, rebellious, or purely pornographic stories. They want to go to Amsterdam and get spanked by a madame in black stilettos, but can only afford to buy my books and masturbate in the bathtub with a glass of wine, turning up the music to tune out the kids watching TV in the next room. They want to explore dangerous men, fully masculine alive men, but not at the expense of wrecking the house that their businessman husbands help pay the mortgage on. Among the five of us, the Scarlet Letter girls have done or written every version of the stories you told us, and we want to write something new."

"Speak for yourself, Alethea. I'm content with my murder mysteries and elevator fantasies," Leah chimed in. "I don't care about new territory. I just want to be reminded about what's happening out there right now."

Both women had hit upon sore spots in the group's emotional weather system, and the mood in the room took a dark turn.

Carrie realized that men in her culture did not think of women this age as sexually alive. They were grandma material, right off the radar in sexual terms. The ladies each had to be dealing with their age and sexuality in their own way, though Carrie thought that Alethea probably still pulled in the odd hot European. And Leah could probably have a choice of many open-minded men or women, but seemed to like to keep a distance. She sincerely hoped that Rose and Carmen found their writing, and phone sex, to be fulfilling. At the same moment she realized that Alethea had said five women. There were only four here.

*God, I hope one of them didn't die!* Carrie thought.

As the door opened for after-dinner coffees and liquers, Carrie realized that somehow, in a very short amount of time, she had developed a real caring connection to this gang of tropical birds. That she really did care about them being happy. How weird! It was not like they were all mothery or anything. In fact the closest thing to apple pie was one of Rose's pen names, "Miss Cherry Pie," the hottest porn character in the late eighties. But they were so **real**. And so much fun to be around! Carrie sipped her Grand

Marnier and probed her mind for something, some tidbit that she could give them in return for a lovely evening.

"Have any of you noticed that dark-skinned officer guy?" she asked timidly.

The ladies looked at each other with gleams in their eyes.

"Oooh, we were so hoping you'd talk about him, Ginger!" Carmen said with excitement.

"His eyes make me melt right here in my wheelchair," Rose exclaimed, a loopy grin on her face.

"To be honest, dear, we had noticed him noticing you, and hoped you would have had a story to share about him. Do you?"

Carrie's shoulders slumped. The only real life story she had about FOYB was humiliating. She didn't think the dream counted.

"Sorry, ladies. I haven't conquered that one yet, nowhere near. When he was in my room, he was as cold as the fish out there in that ocean." Carrie felt that she was letting them down.

"You managed to get him into your room?" Leah said, her soft brown eyes staring straight at Carrie.

"Well, technically yes, but it was the most unsexy circumstances ever. Really. I don't think I have a chance in Hell with that one, though I would sorely love to try it."

Carrie was pretty drunk, and found that she was speaking like the ladies a bit, using words like "sorely." She found that kind of funny, but then when the room was starting to blur like this, lots of things could be funny.

"Carrie, your defeated attitude will not be stood for in this room!" Alethea declared. Possibly the wine was getting to her a bit as well, as her voice kind of wobbled.

"You're a beautiful, intelligent young woman, and he's a gorgeous, masculine, strong, mature young man. There is no reason to think that he would not have sex with you if you asked."

"Asked?" Carrie said.

"What, you mean you've never asked him to sleep with you?" Alethea said. "How on earth will you really know if he's interested if you don't inquire about the possibility?"

Carrie scratched her ear and wondered what she had missed here. She was pretty sure that in porn, even the kind written for smart women, nobody just asked for sex like they were ordering their breakfast. She thought that the art of seduction, the flirting game, the engineered accidental encounters were a key part of the whole thing being sexy. How could just asking be sexy at all? Carrie asked Alethea as much. And regretted the question immediately, when a tipsy Alethea said, "Well let's just clear this up right now, shall we?" and buzzed for the waiter to come back in.

"Young man, it's come to my attention that there's been a crime committed here. It's of an extremely sensitive matter, and I'd like to speak to one of your officers immediately," Alethea growled.

Carrie was not sure who looked more shocked, the waiter or Carrie herself. He stared at Carrie with suspicion, and she blushed. The ladies, however, had slightly concerned poker faces on, with eyes that thought this was better than dessert.

"Yes, Mrs. Porteous, I'll get someone immediately!" the waiter said deferentially. As he made his way out of the room, she continued.

"And, young man, I'm well aware that there is really only one officer aboard who is capable of dealing with life and death situations in a discreet manner. I do hope you understand to whom I am referring?"

The waiter nodded. He had made sure he had Mateo's private cell number with him when he came to work this crazy shift. He was the newest male member of the wait staff, which was how he ended up having to serve this group of fiendish ladies all by himself. The only help anyone gave him was, "if it gets really weird, or if one of them dies, call Mateo, he'll help you clean it up." Well, that was surely who the fuck he was calling now!

ooooo

Carrie had to pee. And fix her lipstick. And decide if she was going to run away for real this time. Mateo was a serious dude, and if these ladies embarrass him by grabbing his ass, or listing their twenty-five favorite words for penis in front of him like they had done to the waiter, she did not want to see how reacted. He obviously took his job seriously, being an officer and all, not just some porter, but Carrie figured that he would probably throw his job away before he would allow himself to be made out to be a boy toy for a group of senior citizens. She knew he had a temper. She felt it burning beneath his eyes. That was partly what attracted her to him in the first place, but also what made his coming to this mad-hatter tea party seem like a dangerous idea. Carrie fiddled around in the bathroom for a long time, fixing her lipstick twice, readjusting her nylons, making sure she didn't have BO. She stared at the mirror into her own green eyes, and replayed the bizarre night for herself. What kind of a man did she want to meet? She had to admit that some of what Alethea described sounded pretty damn good to her, though not very realistic. In her experience all men were either easily manipulated little boys, or wierdos who wanted to hurt her, not for fun but to get some kind of revenge on her just for having a pussy. Was there really an option C? And did Mateo have those qualities? And would he throw Carmen overboard when she asked him if he thought going down on Rose in her wheelchair would be a turn on, and if we could all watch? Carrie fanned her face to try to get some of the wine flush out of her cheeks, and told herself, out loud into the mirror, to "get out there and find out what happens next, you gorgeous thing!" She laughed and pushed the door open, walking in that floaty kind of way she got when she was drunk. The door to the dining room was ajar. Hadn't she closed it? Was Mateo in there already? Carrie felt her heart speed up and she lurched to the side a bit as the ship moved with the waves. Or was it just her? She put on a completely new kind of smile, the smile that said, "This is one hell of an interesting night!" She pushed the door the rest of the way open and watched the scene before her in awe.

## Anne 🦌

Anne poked the raw reindeer meat with her finger. She was hungry for real food, red meat, as the weather was getting colder. But reindeer meat? How could she eat Rudolph for dinner? Anne was primarily vegetarian, but had no problem eating cows, pigs, or chickens when her body felt fatigued or cold. She did not have an ounce of guilt about it, to her those animals were for food, end of story. But for some reason the idea of reindeer for dinner threw her for a loop. It felt a bit like she was about to broil a nice piece of unicorn. Yes, that was it. Somehow reindeers seemed like mythical creatures, able to fly around the world in hours and help Santa deliver gifts to all the good boys and girls. That was not the kind of creature Anne imagined herself eating. But in the end Anne was a deeply practical creature, and the idea of wasting this food offended her more deeply than eating it did. Anne trimmed the meat, cutting off more than just fat. Once it was under the broiler, Anne took the scraps to the door. She felt a strange urge to befriend the ravens that constantly flew around her area, despite the fact they seemed to regard her with disdain. Maybe some reindeer meat will change that, she thinks, quickly stepping through the cold evening air to place the meat in a large tree across from the lighthouse, a spot she could see from her dinner table. The snow trickled down her neck as she reached up into the tree, and she shivered, much more excited for dinner than she had been before. She opened another bottle of the red Cecily sent her, and rushed back inside to check on the steak and have a sip of wine. Somehow she knew she would dream about reindeer tonight, as much as she wished she would dream about the enticing Marcello.

Anne swallowed the wine and sighed, staring into the oven as the steak spit and popped. It smelled delicious, like beefsteak but somehow more red. Ew, like Rudolph's nose, she thought, and brushed the thought away with another sip of wine. She busied herself with finishing touches on her salad and garlic toast, and lit a candle for herself. She was not really celebrating anything specific tonight, just celebrating herself and her adventure. The weather had an intimidating cold sharpness to it, and there was a primal fear on the edge of Anne's mind about surviving the winter here on her own. Which was ridiculous, she told herself. She had read all of the manuals. She had everything she needed even if Ernie did not come once a week with treats and meat and vegetables. There were enough canned beans in the pantry to last years, and every one of the odd collection of fifteen can openers worked. She understood how such a collection came to be. Even she brought three different kinds, somehow as a talisman against dying from the stupidity of having canned food and no opener. There was wood and a fireplace, gas and heaters, water and toilet paper neatly organized for her.

The only real danger was in her own mind, she realized as she had another sip of wine. She had not even been overindulgent with the wine, just having a bottle here or there when the mood struck her. She left Ernie a note to bring some more on the next delivery in case she missed him when he came again. Whether she was available, or busy figuring out how her body worked, or even down at the sea's edge looking for more bones, she hoped he would get that message. Anne was not turning into an alcoholic. It was more along the lines of pleasure, allowing herself to really settle in and feel the good things in life. Simple food and herbal tea had taken on a new flavor for her, and drawing the fruit in the pelvic fruit bowl was slowing down her brain and her eyes to the point where small variations in color were exciting, unusual textures on a banana stem, deeply fascinating.

Anne spent entire days drawing one single apple, and it felt deliciously decadent to spend her time however she wanted. Other days she took brisk walks outside, followed by long hot showers, and more practice with the vibrator and her body. She even considered taking a small mirror and drawing her own vagina, which seemed to her more like a lily, now, and less like an encumbrance. This place, and Serena, had changed her, and she was settling comfortably into the experience for the most part. She had small concerns about the cold, and her continuing ability to manage her time, but her biggest concern was not letting that dream obsess her. She managed to forget about it for a few days, then out of nowhere his face, and his scent came back into her mind. She washed her face a little to roughly one morning and was reminded of the feeling his stubbly cheek made rubbing against hers while they kissed passionately. How she could remember a dream in so much detail was beyond her. She tried to draw his face, but of course every time she had it in her mind, it would run away before she could truly commit it to paper. There was one drawing of his eyes that came a little close to the real thing, but that was all. *The real thing! How ridiculous! There is no real thing, this is a face from a dream! It can look however I want!*

Anne took another sip of wine and shook her head, shaking the same silly conversation out of her head. The fact is that for one short dream, it had left an indelible impression on her consciousness, and she was helpless to do anything about it but just watch and wonder. The smell of broiling reindeer meat brought her mind back to the present reality, and she burned her hand trying to get the broiler pan out of the oven before the steak burned. It smelled so delicious, she took her steak knife and started to cut a piece off. *This is not quite it*, she thought, and went into her dresser to take out her dad's old hunting knife. She was going to need strength for the next few months, more than just what the meat offered. She needed to cut it with a man's knife, a big hunting knife, and feel like she is as tough as her dad had been.

"Sorry dad, hope you don't mind," she whispered as she unsheathed the knife and sliced the steak with it. She had taken care of it since she was twelve, and it was sharp enough to slice thin strips of meat for her to chew thoroughly. *I must be embracing my inner cavewoman*, Anne thought as she washed the bite down with a sip of wine. The flavor of the meat was elusive, mysterious. It was like deer, but somehow stronger and magical, like it had super vitamins in it or something. Anne felt herself getting stronger with every bite, imagining Popeye muscles growing on her arms. She allowed herself to eat as slowly as she wanted to, no husbands around to grab the food off of her plate, or ditch her with the dishes if she was too slow. She would be doing all of the dishes herself, of course, but she didn't mind one whit.

Staring out the window, watching the light slowly fade, Anne relished the peace and pristine quietness of her lighthouse. She imagined that she could let her ears, or her senses, listen further and further afield, without any annoying disturbances, just the natural sound of the sea and the wind. No mental buzzing to distract her from her own slow steady rhythm. She closed her eyes and imagined that she could feel the energy from the food being digested and carried throughout her bloodstream, feeding her tissues with good clean energy. Once in a while she could hear the sound of her own heartbeat. Staring at the trees, she could let her inner focus go anywhere in her body. There was no area she could not venture into, no barriers or closed rooms. It was as if she had cried everything out that was in the way, and now she could inhabit her own mind and body with peace. She wondered if it would be possible to capture this calm bliss in a drawing, but did nothing about it, just remained looking out the window.

Silently she arrived, a shiny black raven, to take raw meat from the tree. Anne sent the raven a mental 'hello' and was amazed to hear a 'hello' answered back, by a voice in her mind but not really her own. Startled, she got up to clean the dishes, and the raven flew off, her wings making a powerful whoosh sound Anne could hear from inside. *How can I hear that when the windows are closed?* she wondered, then backed away from the whole unsettling topic. Instead she concentrated on cleaning the broiling pan, leaving it far cleaner than it had been when she dug it out of the oven drawer.

When the kitchen was spotless, Anne dusted every surface in the living room. She was less OCD than before, but cleaned for the simple joy of it. It was as if she needed to feel like everything could just flow freely in this new home. The fireplace was the only area she let stay a little dirty, the bits of wood and ashes far too numerous and persistent to bother with.

Staring into the fire had become Anne's second favorite activity, after working with Serena's bone drawings. Sometimes she would sit by the fire for hours, dozing off with the arm or pelvis in her hands, and on those occasions she had the most interesting dreams. Not as sexy as the Marcello dream, but full of magic and nature. She dreamed of hiking in the mountains and finding a small trapper's cabin with yellow light glowing out of the tiny windows and the sound of a baby crying within. She dreamed of wolves, and of the moon shining down on a majestic snow-covered mountain, one that was at the same time unknown and familiar. Lately she had been dreaming that she was standing at the water's edge, and when she looked at her hands, they were not her own hands at all. They were old and battle scarred, but at the same time beautiful. Sometimes she saw the moon-shaped ring from her other dream, sometimes a faint light shining off in the distance. The dreams always left her sad, though they were not sad in content. Perhaps a better word was nostalgic, like they were pieces of a tune she used to sing and love. Anne did not do this every day, as she was both fascinated and a little frightened by the level of detail she got in these dreams, smells and emotions that were almost overpowering. But after a day or two away from them, she felt the need to sit with her bones again and gaze into the fire, waiting to see what was revealed.

On this occasion Anne dreamed about blood. She was not afraid. It was not a violent dream, more like a deep circulation of blood going down into the earth. She dreamed of spice, a kind of pungent smoke that reminded her of ancient history for no logical reason. And she saw a man, a man who looked, from a distance, like her Marcello. He had a strong back and was chopping wood outside of the trapper's cabin. His hair was black, and his motions were powerful and decisive. She wanted nothing more than to reach forward and touch him, place her hands on his fleecy coated shoulder and ask him to turn around. She wanted this so badly but could not move, could not get his attention, and suddenly realized that he was a real man, not a dream, and that she was really there observing him, but that he could not hear her. She would not be able to touch him because she was a raven. Anne startled herself awake, only to look down and see a raven's feather in her hand. Her heart stopped beating. This was impossible. She looked around the lighthouse frantically. It was dark outside and the fire had faded. She wanted to run to the door to make sure it was locked, but she was frozen in place, staring at the feather. This just could not be. Tears welled up in Anne's eyes. She wished for her father, for anyone, anyone human who was a friend and not some psycho who somehow snuck onto her island in the dark just to mess with her mind and put a feather in her hand.

Anne's ears strained for the sound of the intruder, holding her breath to listen for the breathing of another. But it was silent, other than the normal ambient sound of waves and gentle wind. The feather itself was light in her hands, and soft. It was the same shiny blue black of hair belonging to the man in her dreams, and this comforted her. She was still truly alone, and once her adrenaline slowed down, she admitted this to herself. There was no one on her island. She knew it too well, all of its sounds and rhythms. There was no maniac out there in a hockey mask hoping to cut her up with a chainsaw.

There was only a deep mystery that made her blood run alternately hot and cold. This feather was a gift, if only she could get past the fear of the appearance. Anne stayed still, listening and looking out the window, until finally the sun had risen and she could see everywhere in the house. Eventually she had to move, had to relieve her bladder and stretch her back, and she ever so carefully took the feather to the table with the arm bone, placing them side by side. Then, she moved the feather so that it was draping gently across the top of the arm bone. Somehow that felt more right. Then she took her father's knife and purposefully placed it between the bone and feather, and herself. Anne went to the bathroom and stepped into a much-needed hot shower. She hadn't smoked in fifteen years but she was deeply wishing for a cigarette.

ooooo

For the first week after the miscarriage, David was the picture of care and concern. He took time off of work and cooked meals for Anne, encouraging her to rest and take care of her body. Anne enjoyed the attention, unfamiliar with the idea of someone bringing her breakfast in bed and letting her nap afterward. It was a good week, considering the miserable feelings she was having about the loss of the baby. But in the second week, David started drinking. Champagne and orange juice with breakfast became early afternoon gin and tonics, followed closely by bottles of red wine with and after dinner drinks. He refused to let her go back to work, and started to look at her strangely. Anne began to dress and undress in the bathroom, unwilling to expose her naked flesh to his disdainful stares. Her uterus had not fully contracted, and the protruding, but empty, potbelly was an insult to his manhood. Not only did she begin to look ugly and fat to him, but he also started to accuse her of losing the baby on purpose. When he poured her wine, he would make snide comments about her reluctance to give up drinking during the pregnancy. She had not touched a drop of alcohol, of course, but she had complained that when they were out for their Friday night dinner, she really missed her red wine. He hinted that maybe if she did some exercise, her stomach would look less disgusting.

Then one night he got extremely drunk and told her the *truth*. That he knew that she killed the baby off just to spite him. Anne felt the blow of his rage like a punch to the solar plexus, wondering where he got this crazy idea. She searched her memory for any time she had shared her fears of birth and motherhood with him, but she had not said any of it aloud to anyone. David was a successful Realtor and vicious soccer player. He had lived a charmed life, getting everything he wanted with minimal effort, including a beautiful, blonde lawyer wife. When he went off the deep end that night, calling her a baby-killing whore, Anne instinctively knew that he was just unable to deal with the insult from the universe. Having something he thought he wanted so badly yanked out of his greedy grasp so suddenly was too much for his fragile ego.

She was also afraid for her life, as he had morphed into a psychotic man, the kind that is discussed on the evening news. *He seemed like such a nice young man.* David was not a nice man anymore. He was furious and terrified, wondering what would happen next, as if his life had been somehow cursed, and Anne was the easy target, the obvious person to blame. He sat on the end of her bed and let her have it, hurling all of his dark, insulting accusations at her, while she struggled to understand his sudden personality shift. She did not feel safe, but did not know what to do about it, so she just sat there, for hours, while he yelled and abused her. At one point he picked her right up off of the bed, and shook her like a rag doll, spitting into her face.

"Why the fuck did you kill my baby, you fucking ice bitch?" She tried to be brave, but that only inflamed his rage.

"You think you're so fucking great? How great are you now, you fucking bitch?!" He threw he onto the floor and raped her from behind, holding onto her tender breasts like they were reins. Anne cried out in pain and he just fucked her harder. She remembered reading a magazine article about women and rape fantasies, and she suddenly understood that the difference between a playful fantasy and this was the rage. The waves of hatred and fury that David was throwing at her. Even his come was toxic. Her body wanted nothing to do with him and she began to vomit after he came, her flabby stomach heaving in painful waves. He took her head and rubbed her face in the vomit, calling her horrible names and punishing her for breaking his lucky streak. As a logical woman, Anne knew that this was wrong, that as a human being she did not deserve such treatment, even if somehow she **had** made the baby go away. But some deeper animal part of her could not stand up to him, could not push him away and run, and she suffered every night for four nights. David continually raped her and told her that he would kill her if she didn't get pregnant again right away. Her body bled and each time her flesh would tear anew, but she could not leave.

Finally, on Friday, May 27, Anne woke up. She marched in a daze to her closet, found her old shoebox, and took her dad's knife out of the box. When David got home from work, already drunk and telling her that he had fucked a nineteen-year-old teenager at the pub after work, and that maybe that tramp could have his baby, she waited. Waited in the bed until the moment he came. When his focus was entirely into his own physical orgasm, she pulled the knife from under the pillow and put it against his extended neck.

"Get off of me, let me get out of here, and I won't slit your ugly neck, David," she said in a flat voice that made some deep part of him afraid. He withdrew and backed away, his selfish rage momentarily distracted. Anne did not hesitate. She did not even get dressed. With crusty bloodstains on her legs, she ran out of the bedroom, down the stairs, and grabbed her purse. Double checked for her keys, and locked herself into her Beetle and drove away, never to return. He could have it all. She just wanted to get away. She arrived at Cecily's front door at 1:45 a.m. looking like a concentration camp victim, and it was all Ali could do to convince Cecily to "just take care of Anne and don't go do something stupid" to David.

They knew just by looking at Anne's state how depraved David had become, and they took Anne into their family, bathing and feeding her back to a semi-healed state. Anne got an apartment and tried to go back to work, while Cecily and Ali spent hours at night talking about the haunted look in Anne's eyes and how they would never, ever, hurt each other like that.

 Carrie

Carrie could not believe the scene before her. She actually rubbed her eyes and smudged her mascara, trying to take it all in. Leah was sprawled across the table, her linen dress destroyed by red wine and butter, candles knocked over and thankfully blown out. Alethea and Carmen looked upon Leah with stricken expressions on their faces, and Rose was in her original location in her wheelchair, shredding Kleenexes and sobbing realistically. And there was Mateo, with his back to Carrie, surveying the crime scene and figuring out what to do. It was a crime scene all right. Even from where she was standing, Carrie could see that Leah was dead, killed by the deadly sting of the scorpion that was still standing on her neck, tail poised in defense, ready to kill the next fool that tried to thwart it's evil agenda.

"Mateo, be careful!" Carrie cried.

He turned to see where the noise came from, and all of the ladies, even the dead one, felt his blood temperature rise when he saw Carrie, in the green dress, standing sloppily drunk at the door.

*Oh, this is good, he really does want her*, Alethea thought to herself, then got back into character.

"Oh my God Mateo, how could this have happened? Oh my darling Leah, my dark beauty, how can you leave us like this?"

Alethea crooned, causing Carrie to pause. Just what were these wrinkly minxes up to? Carrie studied the scorpion, certain that it was plastic. Until it moved, shifting its tail in her direction.

*How the fuck did a live scorpion get in here?* Carrie thought, wishing she were a little less drunk. This whole situation did not make sense. How could Leah have been killed by a scorpion while Carrie took a pee and fixed her lipstick?

Carrie tore her gaze away from the scorpion and looked at Mateo, who was looking at her with *I should have known you were a part of this* written on his face. Carrie flushed under his intense gaze, alternating between feeling naked and wishing they were both naked. This man had the most intoxicating affect on her. Fuck! What was she supposed to do about this? And Jesus, her new friend Leah was dead on the table, condiments streaking across her sexy leg, and all Carrie could think about was what kissing Mateo would be like. What kind of cold-hearted bitch was she? Carrie had actually liked Leah the best, having a pretty sexual non-sexual crush on the Egyptian Queen. And now she was fucking dead, with the evil goddamn scorpion standing right on her chest looking for its next victim.

Carrie wobbled a little as she looked at the remaining scarlet sisters, wondering how they would survive the loss of another member of their group. Alethea looked broken, like a deeply hurt woman trying to hold it all together. Rose was in her own little world, staring at the bottom of Leah's feet and no longer in the room, probably withdrawing into some childish damaged psychological state. Then there was Carmen. Carrie looked at Carmen, and Carmen half smiled at Carrie, gesturing excessively with her eyes and head toward Mateo. Like Carrie should go for it. Like it was all some silly game. *Oh my God, they fucking faked this,* Carrie realized, swaying dangerously on her feet with terror. How would Mateo react when he discovered their ruse? But the fucking scorpion was real. What the fuck was going on here? Carrie swayed even farther the other direction, her inebriated brain short-circuiting. Mateo looked at her with concern, and strode toward her just as the edges of Carrie's vision got funny black curtains that proceeded to close. Exit, stage floor!

ooooo

"Bleaaahhhh!" Carrie let out a disgusted sound. Someone was making her breathe in a terrible smell, and she awoke violently to get as far away from it as possible.

"See, I told you it would work" Carrie heard Leah say. Leah, who had been dead on the table last time Carrie saw her.

"That is amazing. Thank you for sharing that with me," Mateo said, and the proximity of his voice made Carrie realize that it was he who held the foul odor to her nose, and was still kneeling on the floor beside her.

"How are you feeling, my love?" Mateo asked Carrie with a wink.

"Uuuuuugggghhhh, not very well. Please don't ever make me smell that smell ever again. What the hell was it?"

"Scorpion excrement. According to Ms. Leah, it has even more magical healing properties beyond being a substitute for smelling salts."

"Scorpion shit! Yuck, get it away from me! You didn't get any of my dress, did you!?"

"Relax, darling, your beautiful dress is fine, and so are you. So incredibly fine."

Mateo looked at her lustfully, and she had two simultaneous reactions: her body said *oh yeah, this is what I've been waiting for*, and her brain said *why is he acting so strangely?*

"Just exactly what is going on in here?" Carrie asked.

"Let me wash my hands and I'll tell you, darling," Mateo said. He dashed away to dispose of the scorpion shit and returned with clean-smelling hands, which he placed dangerously close to her heart on her perspiring chest. He closed his eyes and seemed to be listening to her body with his hands.

*Weird. And hot, sexy hot, as well as a warm.*

Penetrating heat that seemed to come out of his hands and go into her body warmed her entirely and cleared her fuzzy head a bit. Enough to sit up and say to him, "Enough hanky panky, mister, what is going on in here?"

Mateo laid her back down, so that her head was on his lap. He was wearing shorts, so the skin of her scalp was touching the hairy skin of his thighs. Carrie's head went toward fuzzy again, not from wine but from the intense attraction she felt for this man. She fought an urge to roll over and kiss his thighs for fun, and listened intently. The ladies were all crowded around her, listening in.

"Darling, it would appear that the amount of alcohol you managed to consume, combined with the death of Ms. Leah here, was a bit too much for you, my fragile little flower."

"Ok Mateo, why are you talking so weirdly to me? I'm not your flower or even your darling." Carrie squirmed to look at him, and saw the devil in his eyes.

*Oh no*, she thought, *how long have I been out, and what the hell have these ladies told him?*

Yup, that was it. They had filled his head with some story. She saw it in his eyes.

"Ti amo," Mateo said, laying it on thickly now. "Your wonderful new friends have explained to me your delicate condition, and also your passionate desire to make love to me. How could I possibly deny you anything your tender heart desires?"

Carrie's heart did not feel tender. It felt furious at the Scarlet Letters for setting her up. Then she took in the part about him not saying no, and flames of heat licked deep in her abdomen. Having her head on his muscular lap, smelling his spicy scent, and imaging the two of them together actually made Carrie feel faint again. Her eyes fluttered like an old Harlequin Romance heroine, and she had to lie back down.

"Oh darling, is it your heart?" Mateo asked with false concern. She knew that he knew damn well her heart was fine, and her body was calling out for his skin to be on hers. The bastard was enjoying this little spectacle!

Carrie was ready to throw cold water, figuratively speaking, on her belly and throw Mateo out of there. Enough of this bullshit! Then her eye caught the expression on Rose's face: the old tangerine was so turned on and excited right now! She looked like she would give anything to be in Carrie's place, young, healthy, and with her head in a God of a man's lap.

"You sweet man, I cannot believe you are being so kind to me."

At first Carrie sounded silly to her own ears, but one look at his face made her determined to out-act him.

"My heart feels really weak. I am afraid I may not see the light of day. If only I had had the chance to do the things I wanted to do before it came to this. But I fear my time is running out."

Mateo's eyes flashed and he leered down at her. "Darling, is there anything, anything at all I can do for you to make tonight, your last night alive, special for you? Perhaps a walk beneath the stars, or a chance to meet the Captain?"

*Blech*, Carrie thought, *what kind of a last night would that be? I guess this is up to me.*

"Sir, it does pain me to speak of such things aloud, and in front of my respectable aunties. But I am young and innocent, and it is my deepest wish to know the secrets of the male-female union before I pass. If you would be so kind, I was hoping you would take me out of my state of virginity before I forever leave my state of being alive."

Carrie looked up at Mateo with innocent eyes, and she saw that she had gotten to him. She imagined that she felt a stirring in the shorts above her head, and shifted so that her elbow revealed even more of her perfect breasts for his viewing pleasure.

He did hesitate, just for a moment, then suddenly he scooped her up off of the floor and declared his intentions.

"Though it will be great personal sacrifice for myself and my honor, I will take you to my cabin in the woods and teach you all that I know in the art of lovemaking, my little flower. Oh, you are light as a feather in your delicate condition," he added, after grunting with the effort of getting the door opened.

Mateo bid the ladies a good night, and thanked them for allowing him to be a part of this gorgeous young girl's brave life. Then he strode through the door, just missing Carrie's head on the edge, shut the door behind him, and they both broke into outrageous laughter.

"You were great!" Carrie said. "They are loving this! All four of them are probably writing up their own version of the story right now!"

"No, my flower, they are drinking tea and describing to each other all of the things they hope that I am going to do to you." Mateo laughed, with a dark edge to his voice.

Carrie felt vulnerable, realizing that Mateo had shown her more of himself than he showed most people, and also knowing that she wanted him to take her to a cabin in the woods some day. Or at least to her cabin, **right now**. She looked at him and begged him to understand, with her eyes.

"Carrie," he spoke, his deep voice catching a bit, "I know we were play acting, but could I please make love to you tonight?"

Carrie turned to honey inside and said quietly, "Yes, please."

They held hands and walked quickly to her cabin, the heat between their hands making them walk even faster. Finally they got to Carrie's door, which she unlocked in a second and turned back to face him, reaching up and pulling him inside by his shirt collar. He groaned with excitement and closed the door behind him.

## Anne 🌿

Anne stared at the pear-shaped liver spot on top of Dr. Ross's head as he continued to probe inside of her, looking for evidence to change his words.

"I'm sorry, Anne. I don't really understand how the miscarriage could have caused so much damage, but somehow it did. I really doubt your ability to carry a child to term with the scarring that you have. Sorry, my dear."

Dr. Ross had been Anne's doctor for years, but his presence in her nether regions was more than she could take. Once he backed away, and snapped the rubber gloves off, Anne scootched up the table and closed her legs.

She knew damn well who had done that damage, but there was no way Dr. Ross was going to hear about her husband turning into a twisted psychopath. That was too embarrassing to tell anyone. Anne had not even returned for her belongings, but had sent Cecily and Ali to pick up some clothes and photo albums, and a special shoebox in her bedroom closet. David could have the rest, burn it for all she cared. She was just glad to be out of that hellhole that used to be her happy suburban home. *My God, what kind of a father would he have been? Anne thought with a shudder.*

"OK Annie, I know it's chilly in those paper gowns. Get dressed and come see me in my office for a little chat."

Anne used to love to chat with Dr. Ross after an appointment. It was a rare treat that was always interesting. He traveled the world and had terrifying yet funny stories of his trips to share. Sometimes. Other times they had difficult conversations, like about her father's condition, or the birds and the bees. Anne had a suspicion that today's probing would be more painful than the one she had just endured.

"Oh, sorry Dr. R., I have a meeting at the bank in a few minutes. Maybe next time?" Anne smiled wanly, hoping he couldn't see through her thin veneer of control.

"All right, Miss Annie, but next time is a for-sure. You leave time for me. I had a most amazing adventure in Peru I want to tell you about."

Anne had always been fascinated with South America, and was sure the stories would be great, but knew this time it was a ruse to dig into her brain and find out why she was a shell of herself. Anne was not ready for that yet.

"Absolutely, Nick, I'll make it work."

He loved when she called him Nick, so she thought that would buy her some time.

"Oh Annie, you little eel, slip out my door but don't think you'll get away on me. You've got to be due for some kind of test soon. If only I had my own daughter I wouldn't have to pester you to distract an old man from his hum-drum life."

Dr. Ross was nowhere near old or hum-drum. He was already testing out theories about her true status behind those black horn-rimmed glasses of his, and Anne was not going to give him any more ammunition. She smiled brightly, really putting some love and joy into it, and told him she loved him as she kissed his cheek and slipped out the door, with no intention of returning until she felt better. Or at least less ashamed.

ooooo

Remembering this appointment made Anne feel a twinge of guilt. She had not told Dr. Ross, or anyone, other than Cecily and Ali, that she was going to be away for so long. Her plan was to be completely out of contact, but the letter from Cecily had her reconsider this arrangement. She took a pad of paper and sat by the fire, intending to write a long letter to her mother, perhaps sharing a bit about what had transpired. As Anne stared into the fire, all she could see was the cabin in the woods, and the back of the man in the lumberjack jacket chopping wood. Instead of a letter, Anne described the setting, sinking her eyes into the back of her head as she tried to record the details.

It was cold, and the tree she was perched in, as the spying raven, was a tall, sturdy pine of some kind, perhaps Douglas fir. The cabin was tucked in against the edge of a wooded area, with a view of a mountain meadow. Large sharp-edged mountains stood all around, their tops disappearing into the clouds. Sound traveled clearly, perhaps due to the sharp cold, or the fact that she was hearing through raven's ears as well. The man's chopping was hypnotic to watch, each axe stroke done with confidence and power, creating a rhythm that was steady: chop/split, replace, chop/split, replace, chop/split, replace, then a longer pause while those four logs were gently placed against the cabin's windward edge. Another unsplit log was placed on the chopping surface, and the rhythm carried on. Only after a full hour of chopping had filled in the entire side of the wall did the man change the rhythm, splitting the next pieces into kindling, which he piled in an old metal tub near the door. After the axe was returned its place on the wall, sheathed and hung up, and the area tidied up, the man allowed himself to raise his long arms up and stretch. Anne got a glimpse of dark brown skin at his wrists and the back of his neck when he held the stretch. He made her wish that she were inside the cabin, running him a hot bath and pouring him a glass of wine, with some further rewards for his intense labors in mind as well.

He turned to go back inside with an armload of wood, but paused by the doorway, his gaze landing on Anne.

"Hello sister Raven," he said, in a chocolate voice. "What do you have to tell me today?"

He stood patiently staring at Anne. She examined his face, taking in every detail, while at the same time wondering if she was supposed to somehow tell this man something. She tried to say hello, and was pleased by the mellifluous "gluk-gluk" sound that come out of her raven throat. His face was captivating, dark eyes and soft mouth so much like Marcello's that she wanted to pretend that it was him. But it was not quite her dream lover. The eyes were darker, and his face had an intensity, almost crocodile-like, that Anne enjoyed studying from a distance.

"Gluk gluk" the man said in return, eyes smiling. Unfortunately, Anne's brain still only understood English, so she could only guess what the man had intended to say. He seemed to be telling Anne that he saw her, truly saw her, and was glad of it. Anne felt a surge of love and affection for this powerful man, and was disappointed when he stepped through and closed the door to his cabin. She stood where she was and thought she could smell the aroma of reindeer meat cooking over a fire.

ooooo

Anne awoke hungry, the scent of the meat stirring her appetite. She was also hungry for companionship. Something about the man at the cabin pulled at her soul. She wanted to meet him somehow. It was not as sexual of an attraction as the one with Marcello was. It was more like a kinship and deep respect. She tried to sketch his face, and was mildly happy with the result, especially when she used some of her homemade charcoal to deepen the black of his eyes, leaving bright white spots to show their glittering liveliness. She hung his picture on her wall, and suddenly had an urge to draw another face. She poured the wrinkled remains of fruit out of the pelvis, and took both it and the arm bone to her armchair with pencil and paper. She tried the same trick again, letting her eyes gently roll toward the back of her head, and asked to see the face that belonged to the woman of the bones.

Instantly she was rewarded with the image of a brightly smiling woman, with auburn hair done in two braids. Her skin had a healthy glow, and she had mesmerizing green eyes, full of light and mischief. She wore no makeup, but her eyelashes were naturally long and dark. Her expression was playful. She seemed somehow happy to see Anne. Anne set to work trying to capture the image in her mind. It was frustrating work, but she had nowhere else to go, and with much drawing and erasing, she eventually finished the face, looking at it with admiration. Not only was it her best portrait ever, it was just such a lovable face, filling Anne's heart with joy. She excitedly posted it beside the man's portrait, and knew that they belonged together. This realization gave Anne a deep sense of longing. There was sense of completion, of one-plus-one adding up to much more than two, with the couple on her wall, and Anne wanted that for herself. She could see now that what she had with David was shallow and lacked passion. It was, apparently, the safe option. Or at least until he lost it. But over the years they were together Anne took few emotional risks with him. She didn't really let herself go when they were together. Neither one of them liked things to get messy, there was no place for crying or ranting in their tidy, professionally decorated home. Perhaps the drama of losing the baby and the bizarre reaction to it was five years' worth of passion blasting out at once, like a volcanic reaction to suppressed or unknown feelings. For a second Anne missed David, wished they could talk about her new in-sights. But the memory of the twisted glint in his eyes on that last night gave her a chill and reminded her that he was not someone she ever needed to see again.

Marcello, the mystery man in her imagination, **was** some-one she would like to see again. Anne gazed at the pelvis and wondered what it would feel like to give birth, to actually have a black-haired head pass down and out through the surprisingly small opening, and out into her arms. Or into the arms of some-one she was passionately in love with. How would that be? The idea was both romantic and sensual at the same time. The primal side of giving birth, with the man right there in the room with her, would be embarrassing with a man like David, but some-how sexy with a man like Marcello. Why? Because inherently she knew that he would be so grateful, and so connected to her and the physical side of life, and that his hands would be supporting her, and his eyes loving all aspects of her. There would be no space for shame or embarrassment, only powerful joy.

Anne shook her head and got up to make tea. How bizarre, having all of these theories about a man she had only dreamt about. Anne supposed it must be her subconscious teaching her what it was that she really wanted, deep down inside. And the pelvis seemed to be helping her see it as well, the side of Anne that used to play in the mud and yell with all of her might in neighborhood 'Red Rover' games. The part that secretly signed up for a stripper class, then chickened out at the last moment, in the parking lot, judging her gray sweats as too wrong of an outfit to go into a stripper class in, better go home. Anne felt energized by all of the new connections she had made for herself, and needed some fresh air and exercise to let them gel. The clouds were dark and heavy, and the wind strong, making a new mewling sound as it blew through the chinks in the cottage, but Anne just did her anorak up higher and strode out. She prowled around all of the familiar paths on the island, then needed to go down to the sea. The wind made the hike down more challenging than usual, almost pushing her back up the path, but Anne persevered. The icy droplets of water in the wind energized her, and her legs felt muscular and powerful, unstoppable. The tide was not all of the way out, so she had to choose between stopping near the bottom and standing on a little patch, or getting her feet wet and trudging through freezing waves. She remembered the mud and plunged onto the wave-swept beach, surprised at the depth and pull of the waves. Her tired legs strained to keep her balance as she pulled herself along the cliff base toward her cranny, where she got a raw view of the waves smashing around in the enclave and shooting up six feet in the air. Anne could easily picture, now, how the pelvis had become entangled so high up. She practiced deep breathing, and contracted her toe muscles on and off, anything to keep warm while she let herself enjoy the fury of the ocean waves against the rocks, until eventually they calmed down and eased up on her a bit, allowing her to rediscover her beach and walk on hard-packed sand. And there it was. Glinting, in the freshly lined sand, a treasure just for Anne.

She drew nearer, hoping it really was a treasure and not some garbage thrown off of a boat, some fishing lure a tricky fish stole from an unlucky fisherman. But no, it was definitely a ring. Her fingers were so cold that it was difficult to pick it up, and Anne had to brush some seaweed off of it to get a good look. The first detail she saw was a tiny snake, painstakingly slithering up the side of the tarnished silver ring. She turned it over to see his partner winding up the other side. It was a similar serpent but not exactly the same. The first one had a decidedly masculine shape, a thickness to his body. This one had a more feminine shape, slender and with a gentler attitude. Where they met was inlaid a delicate, round white stone, only about four millimeters across. It was unharmed by the sea, and shone with a luminescence that reminded Anne of the moonlight shining through something, perhaps thin white curtains. The most fascinating thing was that, even though it was freshly out of the ocean, the ring seemed warm to Anne. Of course this was probably just because her hands were so frozen. She tested her theory by opening her jacket a bit and touching the ring to the warm side of her neck. She first felt the shock of her icy fingers brushing against her skin, but then could not deny that the ring itself, or more specifically the stone, had a subtle heat emanating from it. Anne fought a strange urge to put the ring into her mouth, and instead slipped it onto her ring finger. It was too big, and rattled loosely in the groove her wedding band had left behind. Not wanting to risk losing the ring on her climb back up the cliff path, she put it onto her middle finger, then finally tried her thumb, where it fit perfectly.

With a rush of blood flooding into her brain, Anne suddenly recognized the ring from her dream about the arm bone. This was Serena's ring.

Dizzily Anne struggled to remember the details of the ring in the dream, but her mind would not reveal them to her. Snakes or no snakes, silver or gold, size and shape of the stone, Anne had no idea if this ring matched the dreamed ring in any of those ways. But she knew in the deepest part of her heart that this was the ring that had belonged to the arm bone, that it was worn and cherished by Serena, the woman whose green sparkling eyes were drawn and hanging up on her very own kitchen wall. Anne was no longer cold. She was on fire, overwhelmed with elation at having this magical connection to this goddess-like woman. She pulled her sleeve down to protect the ring from the rocks, and scrambled up the path to get warm and have a closer look at her treasure. At the top she stopped, and turned back to face the sea. It seemed to be calling her back, asking her for something, or trying to show her something. Her eyes and ears strained for a clue, but she was just too cold and impatient to get the message. Shrugging the sensation off, Anne went inside to have a long hot shower with her new ring safely encircling the base of her thumb.

She felt blessed, like she was the luckiest woman in the world, and enjoyed her shower fully.

 Carrie

Carrie felt that she was simply the luckiest woman in the world. She breathed deeply and let out a long luxurious moan. *I am quite sure that no one I know has ever felt like this*, she thought to herself briefly. Then her mind disconnected again and she was back where she belonged, floating in the warm lagoon that Mateo and she had created. There was no outside world, no past or future. There was only a perfect alchemical combination of two bodies and souls that had been together many times before, and each sang in joy at rediscovering the other. Mateo's hands seemed to emanate invisible honey, a warm invisible, dry liquid that seeped into the spaces in her body that needed it. For a brief moment her editorial mind had piped up, thinking she was just another conquest for this glorious man. But no, looking into his eyes she saw, and knew, that he was just as deeply drawn into their magic as she was. When he was inside of her she forgot all comparisons, all rulers by which she had previously judged sexual encounters, and allowed his whole being to enter into her whole being.

Their eyes locked onto each other's and they were frozen in time, feeding each other through their eyes, hands, mouths, and sexes. The room seemed to be filled with liquid gold, and Carrie's mind, though sober by now, would slip away to other times, other places, the two of them with different faces but the same fire. They seemed to have climbed inside of each other, feeling each other's building physical excitement and the mountainous peaks of each other's orgasms. Bodily fluid, sensations, emotions, energy, all were both of theirs at once. When Mateo trailed his pulsing tongue slowly across Carrie's breasts, he not only heard her low sigh, but also felt his own nipples harden in response to the feeling. His skin on hers like hot buttered rum, warm, sweet, toffee flavoured. When Mateo came inside of her, Carrie came as well, not only feeling her own insides contracting around him, but also feeling the thunderous exit of his come and energy suspended briefly, then released like a tiger to go so far inside of her that they were one being.

Lying in each other's arms afterward, stroking each other's cheeks, the warm glow remained, less intense but persistent. Neither of them spoke, feeling that words were too small, too cheap and mundane to allow into this wonderful space. They told entire stories with their eyes, traced lifetimes across each other's bodies with fingers and tongues. Skin sliding against skin whispered to both of them of times gone by and times to come, and a place in between where they were always together. Carrie's mind was briefly awakened again when she realized that they had not used any birth control at all, but the concern was extinguished by the love she felt for him, for both of them in this space, and she knew that wherever her life went from here she would be grateful for it.

They dozed off, waking up to taste each other again, then slowly, slowly the reality of life began to creep into the room as the rising sun leaked between the pull- down shade and the window casing. Words like "work" and "breakfast," seemingly foreign concepts, made their way back into the couple's brains as the sun's intensity filled the room with a peach glow. Mateo waited as long as possible before finally speaking.

"Carrie, my darling, you know I have to work today."

She ran her finger across the dark stubble that had sprouted up on his cheeks overnight, knowing that he was the most sexy, desirable man she would ever set eyes on.

She sighed deeply and said, "Yes, I know." She brushed her thumb across his bottom lip, remembering that there was no part of her body that it had not explored, and bit her own lip.

"Can you be with me tonight?" Her stomach twinged with the vulnerability she felt in asking. He saw the risk she was taking and quickly put her mind at peace.

"Carrie, I will spend tonight with you if you desire me to. I have to work a long day today. There is a day trip into Anchorage that I'm required to prepare for, on top of my regular duties. I'll be available for you at 9:00 tonight. Is that all right, my love?"

A week ago Carrie would have snorted in skeptical laughter if a lover had called her *my love* after one night together, but in this case it felt normal and amazing at the same time. Perfect.

"How about I order a room service dinner for us both for 9:00?" Carrie asked lightly.

"That would be ideal. And I really do have to go. Ooohh, you are a difficult woman to leave."

Mateo extracted himself from their private womb and put on his casual clothes from the floor. Before leaving, he reached down and kissed Carrie deeply, with his heart and soul. For a moment the warm glow put the sunlight to shame, and then he was out the door, briskly walking to attend to the responsibilities of the day.

Carrie stretched out in every way, then went to have a shower. After her shower she normally blew her hair dry and went for breakfast, but she wasn't ready to leave the room, and wasn't ready to see Mateo in his professional context again. Instead she crawled back into bed, and put her face right into the pillow he had slept on. She inhaled deeply and let herself fill up with the smell of him, that elusive spice he had. The sheets were a mess but she made them messier, moving her body all around the bed, replaying for herself the amazing night. Finally she got out of bed and began to think about lunch. Her hair was a Medusa's nest, but she didn't care. She found a scarf in her suitcase and made it into a bandana, threw on a little mascara, and went to find something to eat. She felt so different, so strangely content, that even ordering lunch seemed interesting, and challenging. She had trouble deciding what to eat, and ordered a burger, fries, milkshake, and onion soup to boot. More food than she usually ate in a whole day.

When it came, she stared out the window, watching as mountains and trees began to appear. She took ten minutes to eat one French fry. The patient waiter, recognizing her need for privacy, gave her all the time she needed, and by the time she noticed that she was full, the half-eaten burger was cold, the fries were gone, and the untouched milkshake a runny mess. She just smiled lopsidedly and ambled out onto the deck, completely forgetting to sign for her meal, and smiling like a Cheshire cat at everyone who crossed her path.

## Anne

Anne and her ring had work to do. Her position as lightkeeper was different than the traditional role, much less demanding, but it still required some time. With her ring to keep her company, Anne felt more excited about her daily tasks than usual, and did up her shoes with enthusiasm. She grabbed today's test tube and her binoculars, and hiked over to the leeward side of the island, where there was an easy path down to the jetty. It was easy for her to scoop up a test tube full of seawater from the side of the dock. She sat at the end and searched through her binoculars for any signs of movement or spouting water. Sometimes it was easier to see them from a low vantage point, it said in her Lightkeeper's Manual, while it was also valuable looking from various high points on the island. Climbing up the skeletal remains of the original lighthouse ladder was an option as well, one that Anne was still deciding whether she wanted to try. It seemed silly to climb up a freezing cold metal ladder and sway in the icy wind, searching for a virtual impossibility. Maybe next week.

Occasionally Anne was sure she saw a mysterious flash of silver out in the water, but she had never had any conclusive sightings. She wished with all of her heart to find a remaining whale, not for the glory, but so that she could know that the majestic creatures remained. So that she could hear their mysterious singing in her dreams and enjoy it, knowing it was not their swan song to humanity. The health of the ocean had rebounded surprisingly well in the last few years, and hope remained worldwide that the whales had somehow pulled through, and were just keeping a low profile, reorienting themselves to the new positions of the poles, currents and ley lines. Their original migration patterns made no sense anymore, but perhaps they had found a place to get healthy and repopulate themselves somewhere in the far North, where humans were unlikely to see them. It was a slim hope, but hope remained all the same.

Anne sighed a bittersweet sigh, a feeling many of the survivors of the Great Change shared. She was happy that the earth had pulled through, and that humanity had as well, but nostalgic for the creatures that had not. It was a global survivor guilt, and programs like the Ocean Watch Program had been created to help people manage their emotions.

Anne took her precious vial back up to the kitchen to analyze it. Though she had negotiated for her isolation, she had also agreed to hook up her computer connection should her findings be unusual or she had a documented sighting. So far nothing was really that notable. The vitaemeter had given her fairly consistent readings, and today was no different, though the ring on her thumb seemed to make it seem like an important day.

Anne carefully logged her results so that she could get ready for her new nightly ritual. She had become fascinated with the scenes she saw when she fell asleep in front of the fireplace with the pelvis, the arm bone, the feather and the ring with her. She had begun documenting them as if she were an archeologist studying another culture. Her love for the man and the woman shone through her attempt to write scientifically, though. They had become very important to her, and she wanted to know as much about them as possible. Occasionally Anne would change it up and take a long shower, drink wine, and curl up in bed, hoping for a visit from Marcello, but his nighttime visitations were so rare she hated to waste a night on it too often, not liking waking up in the morning feeling disappointed and lonely. She seemed to be able to see the couple at different periods of time. Sometimes the woman was pregnant in a field of reindeer with warm sunshine giving the scene a glow. Other times Anne perched near the window to look in through frosted glass, observing the woman writing in a notebook. She was hoping to catch a glimpse of the cherubic son the woman must have given birth to.

It was difficult to piece the story together when it came in bits like this, but Anne was organizing what she discovered in her unofficial logbook. The couple had been very obviously in love, and Anne voyeuristically watched them make love on their fur-covered bed while baby slept, or before baby came. She also observed heated arguments, the young couple throwing vegetables at each other in frustration at their isolation and the challenges of being a new couple. Occasionally the man would put on a large pack and hike away, far into the mountains. The Woman would cry and pace, wondering when he would make it back. Another time Anne saw the woman do the same, the boy a young man trying to look brave as his mother went away, leaving him with his father, and probably extra chores. Their life was not easy. They had to work hard to survive in this lonely spot, but they had so much love for each other, the land, and their herd, that the efforts seemed to be cushioned with pleasure. Anne rarely heard them speak, so she did not know what their names were. She simply referred to them as The Man, The Woman, and Baby. Once, she had observed an adolescent version of baby masturbating in the forest, and it seemed crazy to refer to him as Baby after that.

He had his father's dark hair and his mother's green eyes.

"He'll be a real heartbreaker someday!" Anne wrote in her notebook, neglecting to describe the self-exploration she had observed. She did not judge him, though. How could she, seeing as she had worn out all of the batteries Cecily had sent her, and they were hard to come by these days. Batteries that is, not well-worn vibrators. Anne was sure there were plenty of those around, and also hoped other women had learned to use them without battery power as well as she had. Anne settled into her chair, with all of her elements in her lap or on the small table by the cozy armchair.

Anne was not tired enough to sleep yet, so she took the opportunity to reread the letter she had received from Cecily. It warmed her heart to know that all was well for her friend and family. Cecily had sent more wine, and allowed herself to complain, just a bit, about her and Ali's interrupted sex life. Two babies did not seem to sleep at the same times, and Cecily and Ali had had to stop so often that they barely bothered to try starting anymore. Anne knew Cecily would have loved it here at the light station—for about two days. Then her never-satiated need for excitement and drama would have driven them both crazy! She probably would, however, have climbed the damn ladder to a good high view of Hecate Strait, Anne thought, feeling guilty for her cowardice. Maybe tomorrow.

The most interesting tidbit in Cecily's letter had been her comment about the article she had read in her pediatrician's office. It seemed that at some time just after the twins were born, Cecily remembered reading an article in a magazine about a woman who had disappeared from a cruise ship. Cecily thought it had been a few years ago, and even from an Alaskan route, but she could not be sure. Anne was well aware of Cecily's ability to garnish the truth with a heavy serving of juicy imaginings, so she tried not to get overly excited. But a part of her felt that maybe she was onto something. Perhaps she would learn where her Serena had really come from, who the woman who owned the bones really was. Though it really felt to Anne like the woman she saw in her visitations of the trapper's cabin was the one who owned the bones, if it turned out to be a woman who fell overboard, or something worse, that would make sense as well. And since the currents had changed so much, it would be impossible to predict where something like bones would end up. Cecily had promised Anne that when she had a chance, she would research the disappearance, and when the twins went for their next check-up, she planned to scour the doctor's office for the original article.

Anne wondered if, should she discover the truth about Serena, it would feel as true as the dreams did. Could she possibly feel the same kinship with some unlucky soul who fell, or was pushed, off of a cruise ship that she felt for The Woman? Anne's mind, which had been stretched quite a bit lately, could only think about this for a moment or two, until deciding that reality was just too rubbery sometimes for her liking.

The chaos of the last few years had sharply developed Anne's survival mind, and it took effort for her to relax into her metaphysical side, especially considering just how bloody weird everything had gotten! Smiling about the wonderful weirdness her hermitage had taken on, she took a sip of tea and gently closed her eyes. Occasionally she woke up cold, having to pee, and not knowing anything more than she had the night before, but tonight felt full of magical possibilities. Listening to the crackly song of the logs in the fire, Anne yawned deeply and let her mind wonder, releasing theories and wishful thinking about Serena, and imagining The Man and The Woman. What scene could she possibly get to see tonight?

Carrie

"Does the land hold the sea, or does the sea hold the land?"

Carrie pulled herself out of her reverie to find Alethea standing next to her, looking far healthier than Carrie expected. The amount of wine the ladies put away last night, combined with their age, would take them all day to sleep off, or so Carrie thought. Maybe even two days. She did not expect to have to face them so soon, and was glad to have Alethea asking some strange Zen question rather than, "So did you two do it?" which is what she expected from at least two of them.

"Um, Alethea, I have absolutely no idea what you're talking about. Do you mean like plate tectonics and earthquakes and shit, or are you being poetic?"

Alethea laughed and asked Carrie what the difference was. Wasn't all science really poetry of life, and all poetry really a different description of scientific fact?

"Sure," was the only response Carrie could manage. She was not being sarcastic though, just wonderfully unconcerned.

"It looks like I was right, again. I am so gifted at matchmaking!" Alethea said, smiling warmly.

This did get Carrie's attention. "Matchmaking? What are you talking about Alethea?"

Suddenly Carrie was suspicious of the whole thing. If Leah could sacrifice a designer dress and come up with a tame scorpion just to create a scene, just what were these vixens capable of? How long had they been watching Carrie? How much of last night was just as fake as Leah's death? How the hell did they know Mateo would come? And who used scorpion shit for anything?

Carrie felt woozy and had to sit down. She wobbled over to a deck chair and just held onto the armrests, waiting for the feeling to pass. Alethea tucked in the hung-over, sexually satisfied, and totally confused young woman with a gray blanket, and pulled up a chair. She flagged a sexy waiter over and demanded two cups of hot cocoa, made the old fashioned way. Carrie noticed that the man, a boy really, did not ask what the old fashioned way was. How often had Alethea ordered that? Why did it seem like everyone else knew more about what was going on than she did? Her head pounded and she muttered some colorful curse words unexpectedly, then apologized profusely to the stylish Alethea.

"Oh, don't apologize dear. How unbecoming of a woman of your effervescence. Now I suppose you might have a few questions about our evening last night?"

Carrie thought back to last night, her mind lingering on the smell of Mateo's neck, a scent somewhere between nutmeg and burnt sugar. Her entire body became aroused just thinking about him, and she hoped Alethea had somehow not noticed. Though she was beginning to suspect that Alethea noticed everything. Every little detail about everyone she took any interest in.

*What the hell have I gotten myself into*, Carrie asked herself again, while the waiter dropped off two perfect hot cocoas with whipped cream, chocolate shavings, and delicate Dutch spice cookies. Carrie felt certain that had anyone else ordered hot cocoa, it would have come out of a machine and been delivered in a paper cup. She took a small sip and tasted the heavenly combination of real whipped cream with barely sweet hot cocoa. It was an orgasmic drink after an orgasmic night. Carrie settled back into her lounge chair and waited for Alethea to spill some beans. Alethea gazed at the rugged Alaskan coastline and waited for Carrie to ask a question.

The two women, more similar than either of them realized, held their ground for an entire cocoa-drinking and cookie-nibbling time. Finally Carrie was the one to crack, her youth giving her a disadvantage.

"Ok, Alethea, would you mind just letting me know what the truth is with you luscious ladies?"

Alethea considered launching into a diatribe about the slippery nature of truth and perceptions, but took pity on the girl. Instead she replied, " We are who we said we are, the Scarlet Letter Society, a self-declared club of writers who support each other's work and explore the world and sexuality together. Some of us have been married, some more often than others, and some of us have chosen to remain single, and enjoyed the freedom of traveling unencumbered. Rose's writing is by far the most pornographic of all of us. Sometimes even I find it, shall we say, challenging. She is also the most fun, and before her diabetes she was the most insane, getting us into ridiculous situations repeatedly."

Alethea paused, relishing the memory of one trip to Vegas when they had first met. Beginners luck at its best.

"Well, I suppose you're not too interested in our biographies. You must be more curious about last night. While you've been showing your breasts and your charming fake smile to every man with even a memory of a cock, we've been noticing you and highly enjoying your hi-jinks. You've not noticed us because even in tangerine or lemon yellow, women our age are at best invisible to girls of your age, and at worst terrifying. You cannot stand to see what might happen to your pretty little faces and perky tits should you be lucky enough to live another fifty years. So you ignore us, or smile blankly, staring past us to see if anyone interesting might be nearby. Don't get me wrong, dear, I was exactly the same way myself. It's a cultural tendency. We don't take it personally. Especially since we took full advantage of our invisibility to learn all about you, and spent enjoyable evenings theorizing about what makes you tick. And how abysmal your relationship with your father must have been. Anyway, I digress. Last night's dinner was indeed a celebration, but we told a tiny lie. It was not unique to last night. We've been having dinners like that every night of the cruise, and your behavior made for some interesting conversation. We really decided that it would be fun to let you know about us and get to know you face to face. That's all really."

"That's all? Are you kidding me?" Carrie said, flabbergasted at the lack of answers. "You staged a death while I was in the bathroom! You ruined Leah's dress. You have scorpions! You seem to know Mateo already!"

Alethea could tell that it was mainly the part about Mateo that was bothering the girl. The rest was not threatening, just amusing.

"Carrie, Mateo is the ship's unofficial mess fixer. We learned that on the first night when Rose and Exotica, the name Carmen was using that night, got a little carried away with the waiter during our private dinner. He was just so damn smug, so sure that we were dried up old hags that, well, I just can't blame them for what they did."

"Oh God, Alethea, what did they do?"

"Well, Leah writes mystery novels. You do remember that. don't you? She occasionally purchases **interesting** plant medi-

cines on our more exotic journeys. When Carmen/Exotica, whoever, you know who I mean, noticed the smarmy prick drinking
some of our leftover wine between courses, well, she just slipped
a little something into her glass and waited for him to drink it.
Which he did. About halfway through dessert, he began singing
to himself, rather loudly. Then he put his finger into Leah's straw-
berry shortcake, and loudly licked it off. He was obviously delu-
sional, and weakened enough for us to have a little fun. Leah and
I offered him some dessert of his own, and invited him to sit with
us. He agreed, taking off his jacket and sitting at the head of the
table. We stuffed him full of strawberries and cream, and tequila
shots, and then tied his arms down to the sides of his chair with
his tie and Leah's belt. It was all in fun, no harm done. But when
Exotica decided to entertain him with a striptease, he got a little,
um, uncomfortable. She was doing a really lovely shimmy with
her breasts at his face, when he pushed himself backwards rather
unexpectedly, hitting his head on the sideboard behind him. Ooh,
head injuries do bleed, and the big baby began to howl when he
realized he was injured. His ridiculous thrashing about was getting blood everywhere, even on our gowns, and we had no choice
but to call the supervisor. She's a rather sanctimonious old twat
who only fulfills our requests because of my second husband's
reputation and last name, which I kept of course. She took one
look at the blood, and Exotica's wonderful breasts, and ran out of
the room yelling for someone to call Mateo.

"We knew he was our ideal man after that night. He came
into the room about twenty minutes later, in that dreamy uniform
of his. He paused in front of Exotica's breasts just long enough
to look at them, then smiled at her wolfishly. Charming young

man. He had to strip off his uniform jacket to clean up the blood, which was lovely for us to watch. I am sure I don't need to tell you what an alluring skin tone he has, or how sexy he looks in his undershirt. He made fast friends of us all when he poured ice water on the waiters' head, a nice way to bring him to consciousness, but much more fun to watch when you *forget* to untie him first! Mateo called him a scoundrel, even though he didn't know our story, and took him out of the room by the scruff of the neck. When he came back for his jacket, we all helped tidy up, then drank some rare and lovely brandy together. He told us a bit about himself, and I believe he may have added one or even two words to our list of synonyms for male and female genitalia. He did not flinch once, no matter what Rose, Exotica, or any of us threw at him. Finally we gave up trying to shock him and instead he regaled us with stories of medical disasters and drug-fueled teenaged dramas he had untangled and set to rights over the last few years. We begged him to be our private waiter, but he told us he was honored, but just too busy to make that commitment. He did, however, handpick our next servers, and they have been not only discreet, but also rather handsome. How could we not fix you up with your obvious soul mate?"

Carrie had been enjoying the story so much that the last part caught her off guard. Set up? Soul mate?

"Let me get this straight. You guys cooked up this whole thing last night to get me and Mateo together?" she asked.

"Well, darling, not to be too harsh, but your infantile attempts were getting you nowhere fast. We knew that you two didn't stand a chance without a little divine intervention. And we are a divine group of gals, aren't we?"

"Hey, who says I didn't have a chance? He was totally starting to notice me. Come on, give me a little credit here," Carrie threw back, rather defensively.

"If you like to believe that, dear, go ahead and delude yourself. But we knew he told many of the waiters that you were nothing but trouble and to be avoided like the bubonic plague. And you were also almost out of time."

"We still have like three days left. I could have done it." Carrie was fully engaged in defending her mojo.

"Oh. My. I just assumed he would have mentioned it to you. How awkward." Alethea sat back in her chair pensively.

"Now what!" Carrie demanded.

"Well, it's not my place to say, really. I have no patience for gossip."

"You seemed to think it's ok to meddle with my life and make me think people are dead. What the hell is a little gossip going to matter!" Carrie felt a sense of dread below the obvious frustration.

The two stared each other down. Finally Alethea stood up.

"Forgive me Carrie," she said, smoothing down the front of her expensive skirt. "I promised Rose I would return promptly to help her with her injection. I feel that I've made quite a gaffe here, and I'm not sure how to undo it gracefully. All I'm going to tell you is *be sure to ask Mateo about Anchorage.* What happens after that is up to the real Fates, not me and my girls."

She held her head stiffly on her long neck and strode away, leaving Carrie in a swirling cloud of Chanel Number 9, and anxiety about her newfound lover.

# Anne 🜨

The Woman and The Man stand face to face, under a full moon. They have built a large fire, and have made hand gestures in different directions, and again toward the majestic mountain off in the distance, its snowy peaks providing a dramatic backdrop. It seems to be a ceremony of some kind, and the woman is very pregnant. They are shivering despite the fire, and their clothing is barely adequate for the weather. The man picks up a knife, its silver blade shining in the moonlight, and Anne feels a rush of pure fear flood her system. She has been mildly aroused or amused during the dreams before, but never felt this emotionally involved. She remembers the day her lawyer called her and told her how David had blown his face off with a shotgun after the world markets had collapsed, and reminds herself that she is strong enough to watch this scene, even if this man does something horrific to the pregnant young woman. He picks up a leather rope, and Anne almost leaves, almost flies away to wake herself up. Within moments she is incredibly glad that she persevered. This is not some crazy satanic sacrifice. This is a wedding. A very private wedding for two—well, three including the unborn baby, and four if anyone knew Anne was watching. The man took the knife, cut his palm, and then the woman did the same for herself. They worked together to use the leather tie to bind their bleeding hands together, laughing a little at the awkwardness of it, then returning to a sense of reverence. They each spoke words of love and dedication to one another. Anne strained to hear them but could not. They made gestures together to the fire, and to the moon, then drank something from the same cup, probably mulled wine, judging from the scent. They stood under the perfect moonlight, looking into each other's eyes and then addressing the mountain behind them. Finally they fell into an embrace, holding their bound hands high above them. They broke apart smiling, and the mood became light and celebratory. The newlyweds watched the fire die down, and drank more wine. When the fire was merely embers, they poured wine into it, turned together to face the different directions again, and then ran together, tripping and laughing, into the cabin.

Once the door closed behind them, Anne blushed with pleasure. She felt so honored to have been the silent witness to their marriage, surely a match made in heaven. She wanted to do something new and special just for them, just to show them how loved they were. Anne the Raven flew down toward the extinguished fire, and stood on the edge. She reached down and picked up a half-burned stick with her beak. She had never interacted with the physical world as Raven before, and was enjoying the new experience. Anne flew awkwardly with the stick, toward the cabin door. Landing at the front step she faced the untouched snow beside the pathway and slowly drew a heart in the snow with the stick. It was wobbly and uneven, parts of it black from the burnt stick and other parts just an indent in the snow, but she thought it stood a pretty good chance of being noticed, provided the wind stayed down. She flew back up to her tree, then flew toward the stars to wake herself up. She would certainly give them their privacy on their wedding night.

Anne awoke in her own arm chair, chilly but thrilled to have such an amazing and detailed experience to record in her journal.

She made tea and wrote down every detail of the dream, smiling to herself about how lovely the ceremony had been, and allowing herself to wish for something similar for herself one day. She decided then and there not to let her humiliating marriage to David stop her from opening her heart to another man, a man who was real, not just a dream lover. It was almost dawn when she finished writing, and she felt stiff and achy all over, but she just kept writing.

She tore a page of lined paper out of her journal and wrote a letter to Cecily. *How old do the twins have to be for you and me to go to Mexico for a holiday?* she wrote, deciding that once she survived the winter here, she was going to travel to somewhere warm and sexy, and look for a man with green eyes and dark hair, no matter what his name turned out to be!

Anne had never taken the Quintennium-powered train before, and she was excited by the prospect. It was said to be an exhilarating experience by some, a peaceful one by others. Earlier in the week, she had gotten the idea of searching the island for activated Quintennium. She was probably far enough north to have some around, but so far she had not felt anything. She was far from being a yogi master, but she had noticed that her hands were sensitive to the 'wonder element', as they called it, when she was around it back home. Perhaps it took a much more finely tuned set of hands to feel it when it was below the top layer of earth, though. Still, it was fun to try, and she did find some gorgeous black raven feathers, which she placed on her table with her collection of what now felt like sacred objects. For the first time in a long while, Anne let herself try to imagine how it would have all turned out if Quintennium had not made it to the mass market, or even been released to the public at all. Along with the vitaemeter and the shamanic peoples of the rainforest, the wonder element was a key player in the restoration of earth's balance during the transitional years.

Personally, Anne felt that the transition was not over. She sensed that somehow there were still a few more surprises in earth's destiny, but she kept that opinion to herself. Most of the survivors were still feeling far too traumatized to imagine more change. This was a healing phase, a time to rebuild, and no one wanted to seek out growth. Looking back, the years between the disasters, and the peaceful but oddly empty times they were experiencing now, were a time of tremendous personal growth for every single survivor. What would come at the end of that expansion? Anne picked up a small piece of the authentic activated Quintennium she had received from her mother in the early days of the change. Had it protected Anne, or just made things harder for David, she wondered. There was so much yet to be learned about the element's qualities, and no one could agree on its true origin. The spiritual school of thought, which had gained a much louder voice in the last few years, felt that the Quintennium was probably some other form of crystal all along, but that the fundamental or Kundalini energy of the earth herself had moved to a new northern location and thus transformed or activated the element to express its new qualities. Scientists attributed many of the unexpected climatic changes with the attraction and repulsion force the Quintennium possessed, but also thought that somehow it was the altered magnetic poles that rearranged the mineral into a new element.

A small-yet-excitable group felt a meteor from a distant planet had crashed to earth in Alaska years ago, bringing the element with it, but the government and illuminati had kept the element hidden away, trying to harness its incredible energy for themselves. These conspiracy theorists were incredibly proud of their part in history, as they believed that a small, elite group of them had trekked to Alaska, found the hidden supply in an unpopulated area, stolen enough to sell across the globe before they could be stopped, and thus created a new world. There were holes in this theory as well, the biggest being one of the element's more mysterious powers. It seemed to cause those who were in close contact with it to have an incredibly heightened sense of intuition, a deep knowing that had a strong distaste for anything untruthful or out of alignment with integrity. How the government or illuminati could have stood anywhere near a meteorite of the stuff was beyond Anne.

She did not believe that it was an accident that David's suicide, though linked to the markets crashing, was close on the heels of Quintennium, and Quintennium- enriched foods flooding into all of the markets. It did seem to emerge all over the world in a very short amount of time, like a viral YouTube video back in the day of recreational internet use. The effect of Quintennium on food, or any natural substance, was miraculous, as was the source of its name. The element was similar to kikumi, the Japanese concept of a sixth flavour that brought out the flavour of the food or seasoning it came into contact with. It was the holder of some quintessential life force, a pure form of life that increased the amount of life, or vitality, in whatever you placed it near or inside of, as long as it was a natural, unmodified product. Modified products, such as gmo vegetables, tended to turn into ashes shortly after coming into contact with Quintennium. Anne wondered if David's paranoid, controlling brain had also turned to ashes somehow, leaving him with no hope, no desire to live. The number of suicides had increased one-hundred fold worldwide shortly after Quintennium hit the mass market, and it was obvious fairly early on that the whole balance of power on the planet was going to shift. Politicians were the first to bail out on the planet. Because of the economic overturn that happened, suddenly everyone could eat, and be well- nourished by whatever they ate, provided it was natural. The most deprived places managed to get enough Quintenium to clean their waters and enrich their simple foods in short order.

There was no longer any market for pharmaceuticals, and the natural herbal remedies were suddenly so much more effective. The final straw was the discovery of both female and male Quintennium, and the proper alignment of the attractive/ repellent force the two of them had completely replaced fossil fuels, and all alternative fuels, within weeks. Air travel had died out just before the discoveries, and so far no one had bothered to figure out how to reactivate it. The bullet trains built with Quintennium had quickly linked the new power corridor from south to north-western America.

Search parties had been sent out into the great rift between the Americas to see if there was any life left on the eastern side, but so far none had returned with any news. Hopefully they had gotten a large enough supply of activated Quintennium before the continent had unexpectedly split down the center. Sailors were attempting to go around the other way at this very time, and Anne hoped they would return with good news. In the meantime, the people of the Western Americas were isolated, and unsure how the rest of the planet looked anymore.

In the meantime, life went on. The remaining human beings reorganized, and only people of high integrity could convince anyone else to vote for them anymore. War was extinct, disease almost unheard of, and other than recovering and building Quintessence rail lines, there was little to be done. A group of citizens had created an Oceanic Healing Institute, and were combining prayer and Quintennium throughout the West Coast in an attempt to rebalance and clean the ocean. Though many species were lost, Anne and a core group still held fast to the hope that the whales and dolphins were still around, somewhere, and that when the more polluted areas had a higher vitae index, they would come by for a visit. That was why Anne was going to conquer her fear and climb the damn scary ladder in the morning, just in case a graceful pod of whales had finally decided to come out of hiding. Maybe tomorrow she would actually see some waterspouts in the distance.

ooooo

Ernie was a great guy, the kind of man Anne deeply appreciated. He was a rugged version of her dad, a man who could do what needed to be done. During the transition, Ernie was the kind of guy who barely noticed anything. While the rest of the world panicked, he just re-rigged his boat motor and went a little farther for fish. He knew how to hunt, skin, and process his own food, and how to survive in harsh conditions. Anne loved that he quietly honored her respect for privacy, dropping off her supply package early in the morning and leaving it by the door after a few knocks that she did not feel obligated to answer. Today, however, what Anne really appreciated about Ernie was the idea that he could probably help her get down from the goddamn ladder in one piece!

Anne had arisen with the dawn, dressed warmly, and bravely climbed the weather-worn observation ladder. She was warm with the pride of her courageous accomplishment. Even the absence of whale activity could not dampen her self- admiration. That was, until she remembered the one basic rule of climbing, the one she had learned repeatedly as a kid, but clearly forgotten. She was much, much better at going up than at going down! After a few false starts, Anne resigned herself to the fact that she was stuck. Every attempt to lower her foot into the unknown abyss of the ladder rung below her made her stomach seize into one giant cramp. It was impossible to force herself down, so she just stayed up the ladder, searching for Ernie and his boat coming from the mainland. She congratulated herself on taking the biggest risks when she knew back-up was on the schedule, though it seemed to be taking forever for Ernie to arrive, and she was getting dangerously cold.

Finally, she heard the rumbling chug of his boat, and craned her neck carefully to see him coming from an unexpected direction. Hallelujah, she was going to be saved! Anne practiced wriggling her fingers and toes, making sure that her nearly solid body would be able to follow his commands when he got there. She heard the boat engine cut out, then a few painful moments passed while Ernie unloaded her box and climbed the pathway up from the jetty. When Anne finally saw his fur hat peeking up from the top of the path, she yelled like a maniac, clearly startling the old salt, who graced her with some very colorful words.

"Well boil me in oil, what the hell are ya doing up there, girlie?" he said once he recovered his own footing.

"Do you think you could help me get down? I'm a little bit stuck."

Anne was pretty sure she heard him say something like "women mrrrmrrrr grmmp" as he dropped the package off on her step and climbed onto the roof and up the ladder. It shuddered with the weight of the two of them, and Anne's heart began to pound.

"Just what kind of help is it that you need?" he asked grumpily.

"It would be good if you just kind of help my feet find the step below and then I can let go of my hands," she answered.

Surprisingly gentle gloved hands gripped her left foot firmly, then guided it and placed it onto the rung below. Anne stretched her cold arms painfully until the foot was well in place, only then letting herself let go of one rung and quickly grabbing the rung below her handhold. Her hands were stiffly formed into claws and it took her an effort to let go and reattach, but eventually Ernie had her safely off of the ladder, then down onto the ground. He opened the door for her, bought in her package, then helped himself to the bottle of rum under the sink, pouring them both a stiff drink and putting the kettle on to boil while Anne tried not to cry.

The pain of the warm blood returning to her frozen fingers and toes was a sharp reprisal for her foolishness, but the rum soon took the edge off.

"So," Ernie said once they were warmly settled by the fire, "just what in the hell were you doing up there?"

Anne stared into her cup and focused on the warm rum and tea feeling in her belly as she answered. "I was reading the *Lightkeepers Guide and Mechanical Handbook of 1976*, and learned about the climbing of the ladder being a regular part of the duties back then, and it gave me an idea to use it as a whale lookout."

She answered sheepishly, thinking now that maybe it was not the smartest thing she'd ever done.

"Oh lass, no one has climbed that ladder in years!" he exclaimed with a loud laugh. "It's a good thing you're a skinny young chick or it could have been a really interesting morning for me! I probably would have found you in a broken lump beside the house, frozen solid and covered with snow! Wouldn't be the first time I've had to undress and thaw out a keeper in the tub!" he said with excitement.

Anne blushed deeply at the image of coming out of unconsciousness with this fishy-smelling old fellow rubbing her naked arms in the bath, and decided to be more careful from now on. Though Anne knew inherently that Ernie wished her no ill will, or nothing beyond friendship, the moment was a bit awkward. Ernie kindly changed the subject.

"Speaking of whales," he said, "did you hear about the dolphin sighting yet?"

Anne's ears piqued up with excitement. She had not turned on any radio or computer, and had no idea there had been a sighting.

"Oh yes, my love, and it was down Mexico way. A keeper off the New West Coast outside of Puerto Villarta saw a young dolphin in his binoculars. He managed to get some video footage of the little bugger leaping and playing before it swum off. Made the

Western American news for a week!"

His eyes sparkled, giving way how much this event actually meant to the seafaring old coot.

This was monumental news, and for a moment Anne wished that she were at home to celebrate with her friends. The human population, as it was now, had been sorely hoping that the dolphins would return. It was about the gentle beauty and wisdom of the creatures, but there was also a superstitious set who thought that the return of the dolphins and whales would signify not only the complete healing of the ocean, but the next phase of development for the humans. Some groups felt that the increased intuition and integrity that the Quintennium had brought about was only a stepping-stone toward more profound changes.

"That ring on yer thumb, where'd you manage to get one o' them?" Ernie asked out of the blue.

"You may not believe it, but I found it washed up on the west beach one morning. Don't give me hell for going down there. It was a great adventure. And I really love this ring, and these bones here are from down there too."

Ernie had been silently studying the clutter of objects on Anne's table, and the drawings on the wall as well, but was far too reclusive to ask. The ring, however, was just too interesting to keep quiet about.

"You know what that is, don't ya?" he said, eyes twinkling.

Anne studied the ring, looking for clues that it was anything more than a pretty piece of jewelry.

"I really love the snakes, and the stone is just beautiful…" Anne trailed off, hoping Ernie would fill in the blanks.

"That, my beautiful girlie, is a very rare piece of unactivated

Quintennium. That is what the miracle mineral looked like right before the Quintennium rush. Many of the indigenous peoples in this area were mining and quietly collecting them before the activation happened. That is how they managed to have so much of it before the hordes arrived to get their hands on activated Quinetnnium."

Anne stared at her ring, trying to digest this information. Unactivated Quintennium just did not exist anymore. It wasn't even proven that the mineral had existed before the Great Change. Did she hold scientific truth in her own hands? How exciting. Perhaps being underwater had somehow insulated the ring from activation?

Ernie continued. "I had me quite a collection myself, traded from an old shaman who lived inland. After it activated, I made more money than I had ever imagined. Then I made even more money from the goofballs who came here in mall-purchased, inadequate winter gear thinking they were the big he-men who could bring home their futures in activated Quintennium. As if most of it had not already somehow appeared all over the world. There was a bit left around here, so I kept the men who paid me well alive, (if not necessarily in one piece), and sent them home with enough Quintennium to get them through the shift. I managed to purchase enough supplies for myself to live like a king 'til kingdom come!"

He laughed at his own turn of phrase, and Anne admired his odd reclusive cleverness.

*This is a real survivor*, she thought.

Anne wanted to ask Ernie more about the ring, but what came out of her mouth was, "Is the old shaman still alive?"

Ernie sat back in his chair and examined Anne from head to toe. The silence dragged on, and Anne willed herself not to squirm or change the subject.

Finally, Ernie said, "If the old man is still alive, I'm sure he's not anywhere either of us could get to. Unless you've figured out how to fire up one of those dilapidated old planes sitting like skeletons on the Anchorage airfield. I do, however, have a funny feeling that you might be interested in meeting his son. Let me see if I can find out what country that fiddle-footed fool is in right now."

Ernie's words sounded harsh, but his eyes and his energy gave away the fact that he cared deeply for the shaman's son. Anne found herself hoping that Ernie would find out that he was nearby. And available for a coffee. She shook her head with a smile and decided that isolation was wearing thin for her. Soon it would be time to make some real plans for some visitors, and for her own return home. Ernie also shook off the moment, and got up to get his gear back on.

"Well, Miss Annie, it's been a pleasure getting to know you better. Thanks so much for getting into a pickle so we could chat! Now keep out of trouble for a whole week, and maybe when I get back I'll have an interesting present for you."

His eyes twinkled like Santa Claus and he swept the door open and disappeared in a whoosh of snow. Anne tidied up slowly, stopping to stare at her amazing ring every few moments. Tonight she would definitely do some dreaming by the fire!

Carrie

Sitting on the end of her bed, Carrie stared blankly at her dad's Visa card. She started to get up, then changed her mind and sat back down, blinking away tears. She smiled wryly, thinking about a game show where you could call a friend for help with the answer, and wished she had taken the time to make the kind of friend who would understand the decision she was trying to make. Her heart and mind were swinging back and forth like a pendulum, and she was suffering. Part of her wanted to walk away, take the credit card and get severely wasted, buy some killer shoes and find someone to pass the time with. A quieter but infinitely wiser part of her kept telling her to breathe, and open her mind to the possibility of saying yes. The last two hours had been an emotional rollercoaster, and it did not seem to be stopping any time soon.

After her encounter with Alethea, Carrie had returned to her room to crawl back into bed for a sweet nap. When she opened the door and realized housekeeping had cleaned the room thoroughly, she was overcome with a sense of loss. It felt like someone had taken her heart out of the back of her chest. She wondered aimlessly through the room, touching and smelling pillowcases and towels, trying to find some trace of her magical night with Mateo, but it was as if the event had been completely erased.

Just when she was ready to have a shower and move on, she heard a knock at her door. A smile flew onto her face--'Mateo!'--and she ran to open the door like a kid on Christmas morning. There was a uniform, but it was just some peon. He handed her a large brown envelope, and then produced a single red rose from behind his back with a flourish.

"These are for you, you lucky lady. Please feel free to call me if you need any assistance!"

He seemed overly excited to be delivering flowers, and Carrie was annoyed beyond belief. She swiped the flower and envelope violently out of his hands, and slammed the door in his face. She had thrown the flower and envelope against the door and burst into bitter heart-wrenching tears. Her mind had a field day, telling her what an idiot she was to have trusted Mateo, what a fucking fool she was to have believed that it was magical at all, and what a supreme moron she had been to have fallen in love with a total stranger.

But he was not a stranger, he was not like anyone else she had ever met. Their night together had been intense and bizarre and the connection had been real, almost tangible. But the *it was great to have met you, thanks and see you again some day* note that was in that envelope, with the flower to somehow cushion the blow, was more than Carrie could face. So she didn't open it. It lay on the floor, the corner curling up as it soaked up water from the broken vase, then began to dry out slowly as Carrie lay in her bed, crying. Finally she got sick of the whole thing, and decided to open the damn envelope and get it over with.

The first thing she saw was the brochure for the day trip into Anchorage. *What the hell?* Then she pulled out a hand-written note, carefully penned in perfect cursive. Her face changed like the time-lapse photography of the changing weather on a news report. How could this be happening?

*Cara Mia, Carrie my love,*

*First off I apologize again for leaving you alone this morning, and having this letter delivered rather than talking to you myself. I have an incredible amount of work to do today, more than you could imagine. I want you to know, first and foremost, last night was real. Every bit of it. You and I are two peas in a pod, two puzzle pieces that are made for each other, two souls overjoyed to have found each other again. Just because it happened suddenly does not mean it is not monumentally real. I felt you coming my dear, and I wonder if you felt me coming as well. Why did you come on this cruise alone, after all? We are meant to be together, but it will not be easy. And it gets complicated very quickly.*

*There is so much I need to explain to you, none of it is scandalous or humiliating, please trust me. But it is going to be a bit of a surprise to you I think, and I wish I could make it easier. I need you to do a giant favor for me today. I will be finished working at approximately 9:00 p.m. Please join me for dinner in my quarters, directions included. During your day today, please sign up for the Anchorage excursion tomorrow. Then take some time to prepare fully for a cold and life-changing day. I am in charge of the expedition to the wildlife sanctuary, and it would mean the world to mean if you accompanied the group. That is only a small part of it, and I must emphasize the importance of being prepared. I suspect that your closet includes far more high-heel shoes than winter boots, but there is a store on board that sells the top of the line in winter equipment, directions included for that as well. Also please purchase a winter coat, hat, mittens, long underwear, and snow pants if possible. In your daypack please bring any extra things you may need, and anything that is of sentimental importance to you. If that sounds strange I apologize again.*

*Please look into your heart, feel the love inside of your heart for me, smell the scent of the rose and imagine that life will be sweet should you take this risk with me. I trust that you will take the suggested measures, and meet me at 9:00 for dinner. Please find your courageous heart for our sake.*

*With love, Mateo.*


Winter boots? Long underwear? Wildlife? What on earth was Mateo thinking? Why was it so important to him that she go on this dumb cold day trip when there was a spa and hot pool on the ship?

Her dad's Visa was almost full, she was sure, after the green dress, and the last thing she imagined buying was a bunch of ugly, itchy winter clothes. Was this his idea of romance? Yuck. Maybe they were not actually as aligned as he thought if this was his idea of a good time. And why the hell didn't he offer to pay for everything? Some sugar daddy! Instead of buying her drinks and jewelry, he was making her buy underwear! What a crock!

Her eyes looked over and saw the single, perfect rose lying on the floor. Men had bought her roses before, all kinds of fancy bouquets, but his single rose seemed to be calling out to her, glowing a deep red, like a bloody heart. And so Carrie sat on the end of her bed, holding her Dad's card, moving it gently back and forth, making the little holographic bird fly. If only she could fly like that bird. Fly home to her boring old life? Or fly to the shop and spend money she didn't have on things she didn't want? Was one night of sexual wonderment worth such a dumb thing to do with her day? Was the curiosity about what this dark man had in mind for them stronger than the urge to return to her old ways?

She considered finding Alethea and asking her, but she knew inside that her answer would be a resounding "Go for it!" Did Carrie really want to get off this ship in three days and not know every possible thing about Mateo and her powerful feelings for him? Back and forth her mind went, as she pondered and listened to the muffled voices of passengers and staff wandering through the hallway outside of her door. She began to listen to them as if they held a clue for her, as if some word they said would tell her what to do.

"That breakfast buffet was lovely. I don't think I'll need to eat for the rest of the day."

"Did you do room 311 yet Mary?"

Life going by, day to day people talking about mundane details that did not inform her decision one little bit. Suddenly Carrie stood up and went to the window. Something had pulled her there. As the Alaskan landscape went by, she gazed softly at the coastline. About a mile down she saw an animal move. "What could that be?" she wondered aloud. As the ship grew closer, she made out the color, brown, and some antlers on its head. Finally they were face to face, and the animal, probably an elk, looked right into her eyes.

## Anne

Anne watched the sun rising through her window. She had spent an entire night downstairs in front of the fireplace, and even though she was cold to the bones, she just needed to sit and digest. It had been a night of goodbyes, some joyful but some harrowing for Anne to observe, though the players in the story seemed to handle it well. The pink and peach in the sky seemed to help settle her ragged breathing and review the evening.

The first scene had been fun, The Man leaving on an expedition of some sort, leaving his young wife behind to tend the garden they had planted. She was sad to see him go, but also anticipating something special. Anne could feel that something good was going to come from this trip. The couple had kissed passionately, then the man had lifted her skirt right over her head and kissed her round belly, ending with a flirtatious tickle of her pubic hairs. He was full of energy and bounded off with his heavy backpack, looking back to blow her another kiss. She watched him walk away until finally turning and going inside to teach herself to sew some clothing for the baby and do some writing. Anne felt jealous of the woman, holding her own flat belly, wishing that she were doing something so exciting, so fruitful.

The next goodbye was a huge jump into the couple's future. The baby was a grown boy, a young man. His back was toward Anne, and she saw that his shoulders had filled out and that he was almost as tall as his dad. He was carrying the backpack that The Man had carried all of those years ago, now beat up and dusty. The Man looked at his son with pride, barely a twinge of sadness showing. The woman felt pride as well, but Anne could see that it was tearing her heart out to keep on a brave face. The boy must have been going off to college or something, and though Anne could not see his face, she could tell that he was excited to get out into the world. He was ready to go as soon as his parents would let him.

As he turned around, the dream flashed to another scene altogether. This time The Man was old, his face covered in hatchet lines and his hair mostly gray. He was sitting in his chair, in the front yard, alone. Tears were running down his face, while his eyes stared off into the distance. Anne as Raven flew into the direction where The Man was looking, but she could not see anything unusual. Just the trees and rocks, leading off to the mountains. She flew back and rested on a branch as near to him as she could, wishing to somehow give him solace.

There was a flash of light, and Anne's eyes were drawn the source, the ring the man wore on his finger. He sat for the longest time, staring and twisting the ring back and forth. The sun began to set, and even Anne as Raven felt the chill come into the air. Finally The Man took a deep breath, and removed the ring from his finger. He held it to his lips, kissed it tenderly, and put it inside of the small leather pouch he always wore around his neck. Anne felt bereft as she watched him haul his body out of the chair, and walk like an old man back toward the cabin. He paused at the door, looked again toward the west, sighed and went inside. Anne looked in at the window, wishing there were someone inside to comfort the man, but it was dark, and she just knew that he was alone.

Just when Anne thought she would wake up and have a good cry, she was shown a scene even more heartbreaking. The man was standing in front of a small stone in the garden, and his son laid some dark red roses, bruised and drooping from a long trip, onto what must have been his mother's gravestone. Anne could see his shoulders shaking, and felt the need The Man had to comfort his son, but that he held back, respecting his grown son's need for space. Anne flew away, circling as high as she could, in an attempt to take herself away from all of this grief.

Both of the men looked up at her, squinting, and they each

held up a hand in a solemn wave. Anne felt such a connection to both of them, she wanted to fly down again and get to know more about the pair. Instead she was instantly awake and alone in her chair.

Anne remembered her father's funeral. Even at the young age of eleven, she knew that he should not have passed when he did, that there was something deeply wrong with the circumstances of his death. Her mother was broken, and did not ever pursue the company Anne's dad worked for for any damages or further investigation of the accident. She just took his clothes, his boots, everything that reminded her of him and put it all in large green garbage bags, which she dumped angrily in the alley for the garbage men to pick up. It took two weeks, but eventually the house was empty of everything that had anything at all to do with Anne's father. The eleven-year-old girl lived on Kraft dinner and became like a raccoon, stealing things of her father's when her mother passed out at night, and hiding them in a shoebox in her closet. She looked like a raccoon as well, deep black circles forming around her eyes as she spent the days at school staring at the wall, and stayed up late at night going through her shoebox, holding each object to her heart, smelling them, doing whatever she could to keep her father alive in her mind. By the time she had them all hidden away, it was late in the night, and she slept just a few hours before her mother kicked her awake and insisted she "drag your lazy ass to school."

Living with the bitterness that overtook Anne's mother was like dancing with razor-sharp wire, and Anne's only defense was to become the perfect daughter, doing everything any mother would wish for, hoping that her mom would give her some warmth. But there was no chink in her mother's armor, at least not until Anne was long grown up and moved away. Even then their relationship was distant and formal. Anne held her dad's knife and remembered something she had forgotten all about. One night Anne had gotten her first period and suffered from having to ask her mom for help dealing with the mess. Anne had no idea what to do about the blood all over her sheets, and had to rouse her mom from a gin-induced sleep. Anne's mom had said some cruel things to Anne, even blaming her for her father's death. Anne knew in her mind that no little girl could make a mineshaft collapse, but in her heart she wondered if there were something so ugly about her that her father had died to get away from her. That somehow it really was her fault, and that her mom's cruel treatment was indeed the perfect punishment.

Young Anne cried long and hard that night, finally falling asleep as the sun was coming up. She opened her eyes and saw her dad standing at the foot of her bed, smiling at her, and holding his arms out for a hug. She sat up in bed and leaned forward, trying to put her hands into his. They went right through, but still felt warm to her, like the air that came out of the oven when you opened it to check on a batch of cookies.

"Don't worry little one, it will all be ok," her dad said, and faded away.

Anne fell back asleep, smiling like an angel, and in the morning she woke up on her own, before her mom's alarm went off. She remembered the dream and rushed to the foot of her bed, searching for some proof that it had been real. Just under her bed was a shiny new penny. The floor under the bed was covered in dust but the penny had no dust on it at all, and when she picked it up, it did not leave a clean spot on the floor. Anne knew somehow that this was a gift from her dad. She put the penny in her shoebox, and got dressed for school.

From that day on, until the day she moved out to university, Anne took care of her mom, making dinner while she did her homework, taking a part-time job at the bowling alley to help pay the bills. She got better grades than ever before, and guaranteed herself a scholarship to do her undergrad degree in Victoria. She had a maiden aunt who she stayed with, pouring everything she had into becoming a successful lawyer. There was no doubt in her mind that she would find a way to make the mining company pay for taking her dad away, somehow, and this drive kept her on track until her miscarriage. She was on a brittle freight train, which derailed fantastically into a heap of twisted metal when that baby died inside of her. No longer could Anne make things happen the way she wanted to, and it was a major blow for her. But it did not break her. Even David's bizarre treatment didn't break her. All of the tragedies seemed to intersect at this monumental point. As Anne sat in her chair, alone on her rocky island, a radical shift occurred in her mind.

The image of the shiny penny came into Anne's mind, and she smiled. It really was all ok. And it would be even better. Anne was ready to come back to life. She stood up with a long stretch and began to take down her drawings, clearing the cottage for the next keeper. She sat down and stared into the eyes she had drawn for The Woman. For the first time she realized that the ocean was in those eyes. Anne knew then that her next step was not just to visit Mexico with Cecily, but to find herself somewhere new to begin her life, near the sea, but not alone. In a village with a community she could enjoy getting to know. She would get a new job, something peaceful, and find someone to share her life with.

For the first time since arriving at the lightkeeper's station, Anne signed onto her personal email, ignoring the overflowing inbox, and sent a short, direct email to the manager of lightkeepers. She would be leaving at the end of the week; they needed to find her a replacement. Anne felt a twinge of guilt. Perhaps she should not renege on her commitment to make it through the six months? The moment she thought about hitting delete rather than send, her eye was caught by a sudden movement in the sky outside of her window. She looked in wonder at the sight of two ravens, flying together and circling around and around each other, dancing together in the wind. Anne waved respectfully at the ravens, and hit the send button.

 Carrie

Time stood still as Carrie stared into the bull elk's deep brown eyes. He was utterly still and Carrie felt as if her heart was reaching out to his, and his to her. The ship came closer yet, and the elk turned his head slightly, gesturing behind him. Carrie pulled her eyes away from his reluctantly and saw, in the lush forest behind him, a female doe and her young baby, who was trying to be still, but his legs quivered slightly as he watched the giant vessel pass by. Carrie looked back into the buck's eyes and heard his voice, as clearly as if he were standing in the room next to her.

"Go with him, child. You know in your deepest knowing that he is your family. Do what you must do and take this leap into your destiny."

Carrie's eyes welled up with the love she felt emanating from the animal's encouraging eyes. Of course Mateo was her family, her future. She saw it in her mind's eye when they made love, felt the future that they would create together. She did not know any details, the where or the how of their life, but she knew it was something she wanted with her entire being. Every cell sang out in agreement as Carrie threw her flip-flops on, grabbed her purse and dad's card, and went out to buy herself the sexiest, warm winter coat the ship store had to offer!

ooooo

She was late for dinner. Her stomach was sloshing around while she hit the elevator call button seventeen times in a row. What if he thought she wasn't coming? What if he just went out or went to work on the bridge and forgot about her? What if he threw himself off of the boat?

## Anne

Since Anne didn't know for sure when another keeper would be coming in, she decided to pack up the perishables. Her supply box was sturdy and empty, so it seemed like a good bet. As she grabbed it and swung it toward the kitchen, a letter that had been stuck to the side fell out. It had Cecily's handwriting on it, so Anne closed the fridge and sat down immediately to read it. She felt like she had won the lottery! Not only was it great to hear from her friend, the gifts inside were precious. Cecily had enclosed a lovely photo of the twins, asking Anne to reconsider taking on the title of god-mother or even goddess-mother. Anne was thrilled, and imagined buying them inspirational greeting cards with money for ice cream when they were older. Cecily had also enclosed a plastic card loaded with travel credits. It turned out that she and Ali just wanted to stay home and enjoy being a family, and they wanted Anne to be able to travel as far and long as possible.

The word "Chile" flashed into Anne's mind. Maybe she would get a lot farther south than anticipated! And the kicker, by far, was the thin piece of glossy paper, a magazine article hastily torn out at Cecily's pediatrician's office. Some of the words had been maimed by the sloppy tearing job, but the photograph said it all. Anne stared at the dazzling green eyes and predatory cheerleader smile of the young woman in the photo. She was dressed in a high school graduation cap and gown, with a rakish angle to the hat. Her wild red hair was sprayed into submission but seemed to be waiting to spring out and play. Anne did not need to imagine the hair darker and in braids, or picture the woman older, to recognize those eyes. They were most definitely the eyes of The Woman. There was no doubt about it.

Anne dug her drawings out of her backpack, and confirmed what she knew already. Even the most skeptical person would be hard pressed to deny the huge similarity between the faces. What Anne saw was the personality, the sparkle that was in both sets of eyes, the pizzazz that she had spent so long trying to capture. In the magazine photo the sparkle had an angry, dangerous edge to it. In the drawing it had softened slightly, and was now a twinkle of passion, sparkle of a woman who had seen some awe-inspiring things, and knew about some of life's mysteries.

Anne wanted that for herself. She had a craving to know what kinds of adventures gave you that look in your eyes, and she had a feeling that she was getting much closer to that by leaving her station.

The article was not too detailed, mainly telling Anne what Cecily had told her, that a young girl had gone missing from an Alaskan cruise. Her father was quoted as saying her would not stop until he found out what monster had done this to his daughter, obviously assuming foul play. He had hired a private investigator, but nothing solid had been discovered yet. There was also a quote from a guest on board who had supported the foul-play theory by describing Carrie as a "wildcat looking for a wicked party anywhere she could find it." The official line from the cruise company was that she had simply disappeared, and that the last recorded credit-card purchase was in the ship's store for an evening gown, which was found lying on the floor in her stateroom upon the ship's return to Seattle.

The girl's mother was under psychiatric care. Anne's heart went out to the poor woman, trying to imagine how terrified she must feel. Anne always knew that the miscarriage had left a hole in her heart, but she now understood that every child born or conceived was a tragedy in the making, and realized the courage it took to be a parent. Anne found herself seeing her own mother with new eyes, appreciating even more the strange cereal box of Quintennium her mom had sent from her bar up north, right in the middle of the turbulence leading up to the shift. Anne's mother had traded some good whisky for some pretty rocks that no one completely understood the value of at the time, and sent them to her daughter. Anne's first impulse had been to throw the stupid rocks away, feeling her old resentment of her mother's distant nature rise to the surface.

Oddly enough, the cereal box changed Anne's mind. If her mom was running a bar full of tough old miners, and still bought Froot Loops, then maybe there was more to her than met the eye. The brightly colored box reminded Anne of the small things her mom had done for her before her dad's passing. Halloween costumes sewn by hand one year, an entire day of baking and decorating cookies one Christmas. Though inconsistent and unpredictable, her mother had still found bright ways to show her love for Anne, and so Anne held onto the funny box of minerals. Good thing that she did, too.

Shortly after the unexpected plate shifts, and the flooding and volcanic activity that came with it, Anne was repacking her most-precious possessions into a large pack, as were Cecily and Ali. She put her hands on the Froot Loop box to throw the stones out into the garden and she was amazed to feel heat coming from the box. When she poured the rocks on the floor, she called Cecily and Ali in immediately to see how they had transformed. While the crystals had been a somber shade of muddy lilac and dirty green before, they now positively glowed, pulsating through various beautiful shades of purple and green.

"Anne," Ali said quietly, "do you realize what that is?"

They sat staring at the stones, feeling the healing rays pass from the stones to their bodies and minds. Anne understood then what her mother had really done for her. Whether by accident or on purpose, Anne's mom had effectively saved Anne's life, and those of then-pregnant Cecily, and her wonderful man Ali. The pure Quintennium was more than enough for the family to get to a safe place and trade for all of the food and supplies they needed to ride out the global undulations and the chaos that followed. Ali had proposed putting the Quintennium in a lockbox, but Anne refused, instead taking clear packing tape and fortifying the Froot Loop box, which remained the holder of the makeshift family's precious resource. Anne cried quietly and sent a silent prayer of love and thanks to her mom for the gift, wishing she had thanked her for it properly when she had had the chance. Now all hell had broken loose and Anne could only pray that her mom was ok, and that she knew how much Anne loved her.

After the shift had settled in, and the survivors had a chance to regroup and make sense of the new world, Anne had tried to get a message up to the small town her mom's bar was in. Anne had paid well for a messenger to hand-deliver a letter and some photos of the twins to her mom, but had never heard back from him. She did not know if he had somehow come into foul play, or absconded with the money despite her careful reading of him, but a part of her still hoped that her mom was just up there having a blast with sexy lumberjacks. Perhaps after her trip down south, she would go looking inland for her mom herself.

 Carrie

Carrie knocked softly on Mateo's door. When he didn't answer, her heart fell to the floor. She turned the knob gently and peeked her head in to see if maybe he was still inside. Two slender red candles glowed on a wheeled table set up in the center of the room. The table was perfectly set for two, and wine was chilling in a stand nearby. Carrie smelled something delicious and suspected that the meal was underneath the table. In other words everything they needed for a romantic dinner was there, except for the dining partner! She stepped into the room and closed the door behind her, waiting for her eyes to adjust to the semi-darkness. At the back of the room, near the bathroom door, she saw a still figure standing at the window.

"Mateo?" she whispered.

The figure turned toward her and smiled, white teeth shining in the soft light.

"Mateo?' she whispered again, not able to make him out properly. His energy felt a little strange to her.

"Cara Mia!" she heard him say softly. "You have come after all!"

He strode over to her and gave her a hug, followed by a deep delicious kiss. Carrie took in the smell of him. The strangeness was gone and he was again her warm, sexy man. She savored his mouth, taking little nibbles of his bottom lip. He pressed his prominent pelvis against her, then pulled himself away.

"Darling, we have many things to discuss. I think it would be best if we kept that part of the evening for later." He winked wolfishly at her.

They sat at the table and Mateo produced a sensational seafood pasta dinner from under the table, complete with salad and dessert. The couple ate slowly, relishing each other's company. Finally, sipping some tea, Mateo took a deep breath and began to explain himself. As the candles grew shorter Carrie learned about his amazing life.

He had been born in a small village in Peru, and trained as an apprentice shaman. His village was declining rapidly, and his elders had sent him out into the world on a mission to not only create an income for the entire village, but also do some work for the planet in the mountains of Alaska. He was to husband the land, care for the reindeer herd, and do some other extremely important but secret work.

He was going to clarify what the work actually was, but Carrie didn't want to hear any more weirdness for one night. It was something to do with some wonder mineral with magical qualities or something like that. Instead she listened to him talk about his childhood and his village, and let herself fall more and more deeply in love with this passionate man. He told her about the lemon trees in his village, and the teacher at school who had taken an interest in Mateo and taught him individually every Saturday until he had nothing more to offer the boy. Then he was sent to a nearby village to meet with the shaman there, who agreed to take him on as a student. Mateo spent years learning and practicing, until the day came that the shaman tossed some stones onto a cloth and said "You must go now."

The shaman met with Mateo's parents and the local elders, and somehow enough money was gathered to send Mateo to Lima, where he would be hired by someone's cousin who worked on a cargo ship there. Mateo, only seventeen and far from home, had fallen in love with the sea. He was smart, and it was not long before he was learning how to navigate and steer, spending long hours reading ship manuals by candle light. He sent half of his earnings home and saved the other half for something he barely knew about. The old shaman had stared at the stones for a long time, and then told Mateo to look for the hearty beast with long horns, and the mineral that hid below the mountains in the high North. It took some time, but eventually Mateo, with his strong English and mathematical mind, got hired onto a cruise line. First a South American one, then transferring to one that served the Mexican booze cruise set, and finally this route to Alaska.

He had also studied the wildlife of Alaska, using his days off to learn about them and their survival traits. He proudly told Carrie that he had saved up enough money to purchase a piece of land that was large enough to ranch a few reindeer, and also had a small cabin.

Carrie thought it was a wonderful story, full of adventure, and she admired Mateo's intelligence and perseverance. That was, until he delivered his bombshell.

"Cara Mia, Carrie, tomorrow is my last day of employment with the Princess Cruise Line. Once I have finished guiding the tour of the wildlife sanctuary, I am going to move to my cabin. I have many supplies there already, and a good lot of other preparations have been made as well. It is time for me to tend my reindeer herd and do some other work I have been instructed to do, work that requires me to be inland."

He stared down at his lap, for the first time, showing Carrie his vulnerable side. She had never seen him look so unsure of himself.

Her compassion for his humble posture kept her from getting angry, for about five seconds. Then she launched into him.

"How dare you do this to me! You selfish bastard. How dare you invite me for dinner and make me dress up, make me think you cared about me? I actually really started to like you, you jerk, and then you do this, love me and leave me with some long fancy dinner and story. Spend one amazing night with me, tell me how special it is, then just fucking take off on me forever?! Who fucking does that?! Who gave you the right to fuck around with women's lives like that!?"

She was standing up now, hands grabbing the dining cart and eyes flashing at him. Tears ran down her face and she stopped herself, unwilling to let him see just how hurt she really was. She picked up her napkin, dried her eyes and nose, and smoothed down the front of her green dress. Standing as tall as she could, she looked right at him and said, "Goodbye, you selfish prick. I hope you get eaten by a polar bear."

She stared at him, willing him to look up at her, to give her the opportunity to drive her fury straight into his eyes. A long moment passed. Still Mateo sat, with his head down. Carrie waited, the storm of her anger abating and her curiosity growing. What the hell was he doing? His shoulders moved a little, and he seemed to be fiddling with something in his hands. Carrie folded her white napkin into a square, breathed deeply, and then backed away from the table, giving him one last chance to look up and say something. She turned and went to the door, opening it slowly while watching his weird behavior. The harsh fluorescent lighting flooded into the room when she cracked the door, and it seemed to snap Mateo out of something. Like a cat he was up and slammed the door with one swift motion. He dropped to his knees and fell against the door, the momentum knocking him off balance. He grabbed her hand to stabilize himself, then suddenly Carrie felt him thrust something onto her finger. It was a ring.

She stood dumbstruck looking at the delicate ring on her finger and the top of Mateo's head. He looked up at her and said, "Carrie, I know this is crazy. If you say no I will understand. I will die a little but I will understand. I don't know exactly how this is done in your country, but I want you to come with me. I want you to be my wife, and be my partner on this next part of my journey. I love you, and I know deep in my heart that we are meant to be together in this lifetime. Will you give me a chance?"

Suddenly Carrie remembered all of the shopping she had done. The coat, the boots, the underwear. The strange detail about sentimental things. He actually thought she would go with him. He actually wanted to spend his life with her!

He looked up at her, his eyes open and vulnerable, but also strong. She knew that she was free to say no. He was an honorable man and he would not hold a grudge if she said no. Carrie took her hands and held them on either side of his head. She closed her eyes and felt his love, felt the part of him that was perfect for her, the feeling of his skin and his breath that she knew so well, as if she had known him long ago. Time stood still as Carrie reviewed her life back home, shallow friendships and confusing parents. She remembered the Scarlet Letters, and the liveliness they had, the sparkle in all of their eyes that shouted out, "I am alive! No matter what age my body is!" This was it.

This was her chance to be fully alive, to step out of the predictable, reactive life she had been living and do something unique, something that was just hers. Well, not just hers. She had this man to discover, like a new planet, deep with mysteries and richness to be explored, tasted and felt. Life with Mateo would never be boring. Carrie looked inside and found a strength she did not know she had. A strength of character that could say yes. Yes to walking right down the plank with this wonderful complex man. She dropped down to her knees and kissed him, kissed him and told him yes with her eyes, with her hands, her mouth. She realized that he had not even asked her if she had purchased any supplies. He, himself, had taken all of the emotional risk after all, letting her decide whether or not to acknowledge the preparations she had taken.

"Baby, I bought the hottest winter coat you ever saw," she growled sexily, rolling to the floor to make love to her new fiancé.

## Anne

"Could you stop the boat for a minute?"

Anne asked Ernie quietly to cut the motor, and she opened her pack to remove the white bundle carefully placed at the top of it. Ernie was used to keepers having reactions when they left, even the ones who left early. He nodded, turned the boat so that Anne could see the station, and cut the engine. He settled back with his pipe and tobacco, making himself invisible so she could have the time she needed.

Anne held the bundle to her heart. She sniffled gracefully, allowing the sacredness of the moment to overtake her. First she acknowledged the island, the station she had lived in, and the rocks she had climbed. Her small beach was not in view, the tide hiding it from her, but she knew it was there and sent it a prayer of thanks. Then she reviewed the contents of the bundle, and the people she associated with them. She brought her father into her mind, and hoped that somehow he knew how much she loved him. The knife and the shiny penny were inside. She felt it was time to let them go, release them into the ocean to be reinvented as she had been.

"I love you daddy," she whispered.

Then she thought of her grandmother, and how her tidy-but-warm home had filled a part of Anne's heart that her mother had been unable to fill. The teapot was safely packed in Anne's bag, but the tablecloth, once snow white and now stained with blood, tears, and charcoal, was the wrapping for her gift to the sea, and she sent silent love to her grandmother. She felt like the ocean sent her silent love in return as a wave of tenderness seemed to wash over her from the water. Finally Anne thought of Serena, or Carrie. The Woman or the young girl who had gone missing. Whoever she actually was, Anne sent her a huge prayer of gratitude for the lessons and life that Anne felt she had gained by spending time with the bones, with the woman's very spirit. Anne was reluctant to let the bones go. She wished to keep them, but knew that they belonged in the sea, free to wash up wherever they were needed next. Anne gave the whole bundle a hug, feeling a bit sheepish but doing it anyways, and threw the bundle over the side. It floated for a moment, then began to sink. When she could no longer see the bundle, Anne looked back at the island, and saw her two favourite ravens swooping up and down in the air currents. She had left them a banquet of tuna and reindeer jerky as thanks for their contribution. Anne expected to feel sad, but instead she felt excited to get going. She turned to ask Ernie to start the engine, but somehow he had sensed her readiness and was already pulling on the cord. The smoky engine belched into life and they made their way back to the mainland. Out of habit Anne kept her eyes peeled for whales, but did not see anything more than seagull and the odd jumping fish, which was just fine with her.

 Carrie

Carrie felt like a child with her big rabbit-fur-lined hood tied tightly around her chin. She had an urge to run down the dock and jump on the boat, go back to the ship and run home to mama. Mateo sensed this and left her alone while he loaded all of their supplies into a cab. Tonight they would live it up in a motel, then tomorrow they had arranged transport to the trapper's cabin on Mateo's land. Briefly Carrie felt annoyed. Why wasn't Mateo holding her hand, telling her it was going to be ok? She watched him load the trunk and back seat of the cab, organizing everything with care and precision.

It was not going to be ok, that's why. It was going to be hard, terrifying at times, and bloody cold. So he left her to stand and make her mind up one last time. She overheard him chatting with the driver, saying, "Don't worry. They will come over and get in the car soon."

"They?"

One of the day-trippers waved anonymously in Carrie's direction, possibly the one who had given Mateo a hundred-dollar tip for the depth of his knowledge and passion about the animals in the sanctuary. Carrie meekly waved back, an act of saying goodbye to her past. She felt Mateo walk up to her then, and ask her if they could go somewhere warmer.

"Mexico?" she said, laughing at his reaction.

"Very funny, my love. How about Taco Time instead?"

Carrie saw the warmth in his eyes, and took both of his hands into hers.

"Mateo, thank you for loving me. Thank you for asking me to join you on this adventure. I love you."

Mateo, her strong, wise, mystical man, smiled like a little boy in front of a plate of cookies.

"I love you too, my love."

The look in his eyes changed back to his more mysterious side as he put his hand against her abdomen and added, "And I am so glad for both of your sakes that you chose to come with me. I don't think you would have enjoyed raising this firecracker on your own!"

What on earth? They had only made love for the first time the night before last, and many times since then, she thought. What did he know that she didn't? She felt no different than before they had met—well, not in her body, at least. The rest of her felt as different as summer and winter. She looked down at the hard-packed snow beneath her feet and made peace with the snow, the cold ground, and the Arctic wind right then and there. She was much stronger than she had known, and this man was going to have one hell of a partner.

"Taco Time sounds perfect, my love. Cheap too, so we can make that hundred dollar tip last! Maybe buy some extra chocolate at 7-11!" Her eyes sparkled with life.

They held hands and walked to the cab, Mateo holding the door for her and seating her in the front with chivalry. He squeezed himself into the back seat and said a silent prayer of thanks to Spirit for sending him this colorful companion to live with in a place of such stark, cold beauty.

"Super 8 on Caribou Street, sir, with a stop at the Taco Time drive-through on the way, if you don't mind." Carrie spoke to the driver, taking the reins while Mateo sat back and prepared himself for the added consideration of having and caring for a baby in the small cabin.

## Anne

"Excuse the interruption, ladies and gentlemen. There has been a delay, and the 6:45 train to Lima will be boarding in approximately ten minutes."

Anne heard the collective disgruntled sigh of those around her in the crowded train station. The weather in Seattle was dreary, rain running down the windows in constant rivers, and everyone wanted to get on their way toward the sunshine. A group of giggling teenagers wearing "Rainforest Regeneration" T-shirts burst into laughter. Obviously someone had said something funny about the delay, and the holiday had begun for them the moment their parents had dropped them off at the station. Anne was fine of course, she was used to waiting, now. Since Ernie's suggestion that she explore Peru and Lima she had been in a flurry of preparations. When she was finally ready she had arrived at the station early, and settled in with a large tea. She was spending time with the characters in her sketchbook, looking into their eyes and learning more about them. She needed some time to recover from the sadness of her dream the night before. She had experienced something through someone else's eyes that had left her dazed and confused when the alarm went off to get ready to get on the train. Anne turned her book to The Woman's page, and looked tenderly into The Woman's sparkly eyes, allowing herself to remember that last dream.

When Anne first entered into this powerful dream, she felt uncomfortable. She was seeing through eyes that were not her own again, and did not belong to Raven, either. All of the sensations in this dream were far more intense than any other dream she had had. It was as if she were melding with another person, yet she still held onto her own consciousness as well. The body she was within felt old and brittle, low on life energy and full of pain. The feet and hands were frozen; all of the joints ached with cold and exhaustion. The pain was surprisingly easy to ignore, however, as there was so much to see and feel. Anne looked down and saw worn boots standing at the edge of the ocean. In front of her was a vast and wild sea, gray waves crashing up to the shore. The body turned around to look behind her, and Anne saw the most majestic sight. Giant mountains loomed in the moonlit distance, and the entire sky was full of sheets of dancing lights. Purple, green, pink, every color of the rainbow shimmered above her, and there almost seemed to be friendly faces coming and going in and out of the colors. Anne looked at the chest area and saw a multicolored glowing strand of light that went from the heart back into the mountains. When she imagined its journey, she saw that it connected to an old man sitting in a chair in front of a cabin. A very familiar cabin. Anne knew with certainty that she had been blessed with the opportunity to see through The Woman's eyes. The pelvis she could feel within the body was the same pelvis that Anne had communed with, and thrown back to the sea only yesterday. The arm was there too, a strong right forearm that had carried a baby and written scores of fun novels to pass the time.

Denene Derksen

There was another band of glowing light going from the heart to the far right, at its end was a wonderful grown man who the pelvis had carried then allowed to pass into this world, then set free to follow his own destiny.

It was all inside of her now. Anne was inside of The Woman, of Carrie, and she knew everything, felt everything. Details of Carrie's past played out for both of them. Together they felt the waves of emotion that accompanied the memories. Why was Carrie standing alone at the edge of the sea, half frozen and exhausted, but full of a quiet joy? Slowly it dawned on Anne that she was here to witness the end of Carrie's life. She felt briefly the pain of a failing heart, a deep defect that Mateo had not been able, or even willing, to repair despite his incredible training. Together they felt Mateo's love coming down the cord of light, sending Carrie the strength to find her ending as she wanted it. Anne felt the deep sense of satisfaction Carrie held, knowing that with her writing, her mothering of Marcello and loving of Mateo, and this final step, that she had truly fulfilled her highest life path. The women turned to face the sea, and the full moon shining above it. In the distance they could see a pod of whales who had come out for the occasion, their song calling Carrie home. Anne looked at the whales with joy, their giant grace a deep comfort to her. Anne felt Carrie say goodbye to her life, then begin walking farther into the ice-cold water, but not feeling anything but love, joy, and release.

Together they walked into the thrashing sea, until water was washing over their heads. Anne was afraid, even if Carrie was not. Then Anne heard Carrie's voice in her own mind, clearly telling her, "Don't be afraid, Anne. The grandmothers will always be there for you. Thank you for honoring me by accompanying me on this part of my journey. I will see you again soon. Don't forget to give Marcello my ring."

The rational part of Anne's mind screeched like a long nail being pulled from a dry two by four, but she tuned it out and focused on the love she felt for this woman, this stranger who was also like a wise-yet-fun sister. Anne felt Carrie inhale deeply one last time, and then exhale with gratitude for all that her lifetime had held. She stepped forward into the sea and her heart took her toward the pod of grey whales in the distance.

Anne woke up suddenly, alone and cold despite being snugly tucked into her hotel bed. She was overcome by emotion and held onto the ring on her thumb with all of her might, vowing to never take it off, then remembering that she was actually meant to give it away. The Quintennium stone seemed to have taken on a slight glow, nothing like the luminescence that an activated stone would have had, but a warm glow like moonlight on a hot summer night. Anne took great comfort in the glowing warmth of the ring, and eventually cried out the last of her tears and fell into a gentle sleep until morning.

ooooo

Anne mumbled a blurry "thank you" into the phone after the wake-up call, though she realized afterward that it was probably a computer voice. She stumbled into the shower and only then did she remember the dream. In the water of the shower, the ring seemed to glow even more than last night, and she knew it was true. All of it. She dressed quickly and got to the train station, anxious to get down south to Peru and see just who would be getting her ring.

ooooo

"Excuse me miss, I believe that you dropped this?" a soft voice said, startling Anne out of her reverie. She gripped her sketchbook tightly and looked up to see a young man from the "Rainforest Regenerators" holding his hand out to her. Judging from the slightly dirty look one of the teenage girls was giving Anne, this must have been the guy who made the funny joke, and the girl was not impressed that Anne had taken his attention away from her and her friends. Anne looked down into the outstretched hand, a man's hand with elegant long fingers. There was a shiny penny in it. No. There was HER shiny penny in it, the one from her father.

The same one that was wrapped in the bundle she had released into the sea.

It was impossible. Anne swiped the penny out of his hand faster than Kung Fu could ever grab a grasshopper, and she heard her benefactor chuckle gently. Anne turned the penny over and, of course, it was marked 1989, exactly the same date as her penny, and it was exactly the same grade of shininess. She held the penny and forgot to breathe.

"I didn't realize that anyone still valued coins so much, Miss!" the young man said kindly. "I just saw it tumble out of your hand when you were sleeping and thought you might want it back! I'm so sorry if I disturbed you!"

The voice was rich and sweet, like real old-fashioned hot cocoa, like the dark liquid left at the bottom of the mug. Anne felt herself wishing that he was her age, that maybe they could go for a drink sometime. Too bad he was just a kid. She looked up to his face to thank him for his kindness, and was jolted to her core to recognize his eyes. She had drawn those eyes. In fact they were in her sketchbook, right here in her lap. The air crackled with electricity as the two stared at each other, suspended in some deep recognition. Anne felt an energy coming from him, a sense of wonder that was not just coming from her side of the exchange. After a moment the young man looked down at Anne's drawing, open on her lap. He inhaled sharply and sat immediately in the chair beside Anne.

"Madre de Dios," he muttered.

The youth group began to get bored of watching the exchange, and a few of them went off to buy a snack. The jealous girl gave Anne one last glare, then went back to gossiping with her girlfriends about the boys who had walked jauntily off for junky snacks to impress the girls with. The girl sensed what Anne and the young man did not yet realize, that the young man was simply no longer available. Oh well, he was too old for her anyway.

Anne and the man sat in silence, she studying his face, he studying his mother's face on Anne's sketchbook page. There were no words for the miracle they were both experiencing. Reality shortly interrupted the moment when the train to Lima was announced to be ready for pre-boarding.

The understanding that time was threatening to take them away from each other set them both to talking excitedly at the same time.

"Please tell me you're going all the way to Lima. My name is

Mark and I need to ask you some strange questions," the young man said while Anne simultaneously said, "My name is Anne and I think I might have something for you, maybe, and thanks for the penny, though I have no idea how it ended up on the floor, and are you getting on the train? 'cause I am and it would be great if we could maybe have dinner and talk for awhile??!"

Weeks alone and mysterious events seemed to have broken some kind of dam in Anne. Her words just tumbled out like a waterfall. They smiled at each other as they registered the key points in their speeches. They were indeed both getting on the same train, and yes they would certainly have to meet for dinner. A mild shock seemed to pass between them as they shook hands awkwardly and promised to meet in the dining car in thirty minutes. Mark was the chaperone for the youth group, and was required to ensure that they all boarded safely, and that they had all of their stuff with them as well. He also needed to double check that his freight had been checked through. Anne didn't have anything much else to do than remember to breathe, get on the train, and try to hang onto the last bit of her sane mind, while simultaneously allowing her whimsical mind to wonder if maybe, somehow, Mark was short for Marcello?

Mark was, indeed, short for Marcello. Marcello found it much easier to call himself Mark than to try to explain himself over and over again. No, I am not Italian. I am half Peruvian, half American Irish, and my parents named me Marcello because they were living in an isolated cabin in Alaska and when my mom got depressed or tired, my dad would rent "La Dolce Vida" for them to watch on an old laptop he had traded some skins for. The movie always cheered my mom up, which made life better for everyone, so they named me Marcello to keep my mom cheery. Anne sensed that Mark had already told her more of the story than he usually told anyone, by the look of mild surprise in his eyes as he heard himself ramble on. Anne noticed the lines around the green eyes he inherited from his mom, and realized that he was a lot older than she had originally thought. She also sensed that he was deeply lonely. Whatever he had been doing since leaving his parents required a bright sunny disposition, which he could manage quite easily, but Anne sensed an isolation deep within him, a need to talk about deeper subjects with someone who would understand them. She wished dearly to be that person. As much as she was curious to learn more about his parents' lives, and his life, she felt that it was more important that he could be somehow supported by her right now. Without a second thought she reached down and took off her ring, which she had kept hidden from him until now.

"Mark, Marcello, I don't understand much of this at all, but I want you to have this. It is very special to me, and the person it came from is one of the most loving and wonderfully alive people I have ever had the privilege of knowing. I know she would want you to have this now."

Marcello sat frozen in his seat, not able to take the ring from Anne's outstretched hand. He just stared at it, and soon quiet tears were running down his cheeks. Anne's heart went out to him. She took his sensual hand and placed the ring in his palm, wrapping his fingers around the ring for him. The intensity and intimacy of the moment would have sent the old Anne mumbling back to her seat. The new Anne was able to just be with this sweet man for as long as he needed. She watched the scenery go by the window, enjoying the shade of green that only the Pacific Northwest can create, rich, full, lively green. She felt him stir once or twice, but let him sit in silence until finally he cleared his throat and whispered to her:

"Anne, you've saved my life. You have no idea the depth of loneliness and despair I've been struggling with for these last few months. I'm alone in the world, and a little lost regarding my place within it. I was raised in isolation, and I find it difficult to make friends who could understand what I'm about. I'm most happy in the rainforest, so that's why I'm a guide there for the restoration project. But I've been told that I have to leave this position and go to Lima, with some very important materials. I don't know anyone in Lima, only that I'm to meet a cousin of my father's at the dockyards. I have wished so hard to be back home, with my parents, where things were simple. Please don't judge me a coward. I don't know, or even need to understand, how it is that you came to have my mother's wedding ring. Getting this ring from you today has solidified whatever was quivering in my soul, and for that I am eternally grateful to you."

Anne felt the gratitude come from Mark, and also sensed the strength the gentle man carried within. She knew his journey had been a difficult one, and did not judge him at all. In fact she admired his courage and beauty, but did not know how to tell him that. Instead she had a sip of wine and smiled warmly at him.

She reminded him of an owl, full of grace and wisdom, but also the ability to be a vicious hunter should the need present itself. Her abdomen pulsed with the memory of the sensual dreams she had had about Marcello, and she blushed and looked down at her wine, not wanting to give herself away. Instead she took the shiny penny out of her pocket. She told him how she had given the coin back to the sea, and had no idea how it had gotten back into her sleeping hand.

"Even Houdini would have been impressed," she joked.

With her second glass of wine, Anne told Marcello the history of the penny, and why she was also eternally grateful to him, as regaining the penny felt like regaining her connection to her dad. They were connected forever. Anne then looked into Marcello's eyes and found that he was listening to her with intelligent interest, with an added glimmer of attraction on the side. He prompted her to tell him more, so she talked slowly and softly, letting him know about her adventure on the island, only leaving out the parts about her sensual dreams about him. The dining car emptied out, and Anne paid the bill while Marcello was in the restroom, suspecting correctly that he was on a much tighter budget than she was. The wait staff left for the night, and Anne tipped them exorbitantly, to allow her and Marcello to stay in the dining car. Anne was in no hurry. She knew Marcello needed time to get to know her. But she was not about to shortchange them on any opportunity to connect. When he returned, she asked him if he would like to call it a night, maybe have a coffee in the morning?

"Anne," he said, in a voice like honey and ginger, "I've been waiting to meet you my entire life. What makes you think I'm going to let you get away from me that easily?"

She melted into his eyes and took his hand into hers. Together they held the ring, Carrie's ring, his mother's ring, and she told him the rest of her story. Well, the part that was complete. They both knew that Anne and Marcello's story was only beginning.

## 🦋 Epilogue 🌿

Anne awoke from a catnap to hear Marcello returning from his trip into town. She had felt that he needed to buy a few more things, and that maybe there was something in the mail for them. When he came into the cabin, stomping snow off of his boots and unwinding the thick scarf from around his head, Anne could see that she had been right. Right about a package coming, and right about this man. Getting to know Marcello had been like the old advertisements for chocolate bars, a sweet rich experience that was hers to savor. He had the strength and joy of his mother, combined with the depth and intelligence of his father. As well as that, he had, over time, shown Anne that he had a leonine ability to enjoy her, an ability to turn their time together into a banquet of pleasure. Whether they were making love or playing canasta, Marcello gave everything a caramel glow, in Anne's opinion. She stretched and got off of the couch, brushing snow off of his hat so she could kiss him. Her belly made it difficult to reach his lips, but not impossible, and she kissed him long and hard, tasting his sweetness. The baby squirmed inside of her. It seemed that the little one was glad to see her daddy. They shared a cup of tea, poured oh-so-carefully from her grandmother's teapot, and looked through the package together. Marcello read her the letter from his father's village in Peru, updating them on the infrastructure that was being built with the resources Marcello had provided them, one final, giant box of activated Quintennium his father had spent years collecting in this very cabin, then charged Marcello with delivering to the village. It had been a trip that

Anne had gotten to join him on, and enjoyed immensely, especially the part where they got married by the elders in a beautiful sacred valley. Their honeymoon was the long trip back to his parents' homestead in Alaska.

Anne was delighted to see what the last remaining Scarlet Letter had sent the couple. Leave it to Toni, Leah's lovely daughter, who had carried the tradition on with Carrie, to send both baby clothes and sex toys in the same box. There was a good supply of chocolate, and some rum, which Toni insisted would help Anne's milk come in. There was also a copy of each of Carrie's books for Anne to read, and the latest in Toni's long line of erotic mysteries. Cecily had also written, giving Anne and Marcello a long list of birthing do's and don'ts. Marcello refilled Anne's tea as she dug down into the bottom of Marcellos' backpack, hoping for more chocolate. Instead she found a letter to Carrie's parents. Apparently it had ended up in the dead letter office in Seattle, only recently discovered and resent to the post office in town. Anne and Marcello cried together as they read his mother's words. She had written to her parents, telling them all about her life in Alaska. There was even a small photo of Marcello as a baby enclosed. It was heart-breaking to think that Carrie's mom had never received the letter, but also wonderful to connect with Carrie again, through her words to her mom.

Anne felt the contractions increase in intensity, her belly tightening and hurting her back more than before. She figured this was as good a time as any to inform Marcello that he'd better boil some water, his daughter was on the way. She had fallen asleep feeling afraid, terrified actually, about giving birth alone in the cabin, with only her handsome husband to guide her through the process. But now the letter reminded her of something Carrie had said in the dream. Not to be afraid and to remember that the grandmothers would be there.

Anne dashed to the bathroom as she felt a hot rush of fluid pour down her legs. The cabin became a frenzy of activity as Marcello paced and made tea, boiled water and rearranged clean towels. Anne growled like a bear, allowing herself the freedom to express the incredible pain however the hell she wanted to. She could tell it was scaring Marcello a little, but he was on his own in that regard. Anne needed to be free to do what she needed to and not worry about him. At one point she seemed to be dropping in and out of consciousness, and after sixteen hours she hit some kind of a wall and cried hysterically.

Marcello **did** look afraid now, and she lost her confidence. Her body was lost in a world of pain and it was completely out of control. What if her body wasn't actually healthy enough to give birth safely? What if she died in labor? Anne cried and begged Marcello to do something, anything, to make the pain stop. He checked his notes, and it seemed that everything was going how it was supposed to, just taking longer than usual. He peered at Anne's belly and saw it shrink down in size, hard as a rock while she squeezed the life out of his hand and screamed bloody murder. He comforted her as best as he could, rubbing the cream Toni had sent on her labia, hoping it would help the flesh to stretch the way it was meant to. Everything was red and swollen, and Marcello thought he could see the baby's head crowning, but Anne called him back to her side.

"Make it stop. I can't do it. I'm going to die!" she wailed like an animal in death throes, and Marcello prayed for help.

He held the back of Anne's precious sweaty head and leaned her forward, trusting some instinct from deep inside. Her took her hands and reached them around, toward the middle of her writhing legs. They both looked down at the same second and were astonished to see both Carrie and the mothers of Carrie and Anne standing at Anne's feet. They were humming and crooning comforting sounds, coaxing the baby through the tunnel, and encouraging the sweet new life to be brave and come out into this new world. Anne and Marcello cried with joy, knowing that they were being taken care of.

Marcello sat behind Anne, holding her back up so she could watch her mother, and his mother and grandmother work together to bring their daughter into the world. They saw a never-ending line of grandmothers behind their mothers as well. Anne's cries of pain were but a memory, the wonderment of the ethereal company taking her far from the pain and panic. She smiled at the mothers in thanks, and told Marcello to go catch his daughter.

Anne gave it everything she had and more, and was rewarded to hear Marcello cry out, "you've done it!" and then feel the warm liquid form of her daughter placed at her breast. She was overwhelmed with joy to feel this living thing, so recently her inner companion, take its wee mouth and try to suckle at her breast. Anne brushed the blood and mucus out of the way as best she could, and helped the little one to nurse, covering her with clean towels and waiting for Marcello to cut the cord.

Marcello pulled his hunting knife out of its sheath. It looked nothing like Anne's father's knife, but somehow it felt similar. Marcello looked at Anne with an ocean of love in his eyes, and cut powerfully through the thick cord, trusting Anne to be able to keep this beautiful baby girl fed and warm on the outside of her body now. He tied off the cord, helped Anne deliver the placenta, then made the herbal tea he was meant to give her to help her uterus contract. Mother and baby were locked together, and Marcello realized he was the luckiest man in the world.

He climbed into bed with his family and gently stroked Anne's face as she taught herself how to feed the baby. There was silence as the baby struggled to breathe, struggled with the idea of sucking nourishment from a breast, it's lifeline cut and tied off. The grandmothers sang an encouraging song, and finally little Penny drank from her mother's breast. She nursed for a minute, then pulled away to give a hearty cry. "I am here, on this new earth, and glad of it!" the baby seemed to say.

Marcello took her for the first time, and gently cleaned her off. He wrapped her in bright red cotton and gave her back to an exhausted and exhilarated Anne. The two of them, his two girls, fell fast asleep together and Marcello set about cleaning up and making his offering of thanks to the earth, as his father had taught him long ago. He put some buffalo stew on to warm for when Anne woke up, and looked in his backpack for the ingredients he had purchased for the offering. There was a small soft deerskin, which he trimmed down to size, saving the extra pieces to make Penny her own medicine pouch with. He placed her placenta carefully in the center of the skin, and then surrounded it with small things he had picked up in town, some chocolate Anne had been unable to search out, some shiny stones he liked, ribbons, sugar, tobacco, some of the rum Toni had sent, and some rose petals his mother had treasured, which were almost powdered by now, and had lived in a small jar in her bedside table for years.

Finally he added the shiny penny that had brought him and Anne together. She had agreed ahead of time to put it into Penny's bundle. He tied it all together with ribbon and placed it by the door. Marcello took one last long look at his wife and child, sleeping soundly in the bed. He noticed he had not done a very good job of cleaning the baby off, and decided to also heat some water for her first bath soon. He watched the tiny child's chest rise and fall, and suddenly her eyes opened and looked directly into his. He wondered if every father felt this way, unbelievable love and determination to protect this child and raise her right. When he looked into Penny's eyes he felt he was looking directly to the stars, directly into some undiscovered galaxy. He smiled at her and chastised himself for his brief but palpable moments of doubt. Penny seemed to smile back, then dozed back off to dreamland with her mother. Marcello took his cue, and went to put on his snow gear and take the bundle outside.

The sun was just rising in the distant east, and Marcello nodded in Grandfather Sun's direction, holding his bundle to his heart. He walked across the front yard area, over to the large trees at the edge of the forest where his father was buried. Marcello looked at the marker he had carved of wood to mark his father's resting place, and apologized mentally for doubting his father's words. Long ago Mateo had taught Marcello about the prophecies, how the north and the south needed to connect in order for the earth to birth a new species of mankind, and how the Quintennium he spent his life mining was vital to all of mankind. He had charged Marcello with the responsibility of taking the rest of the family's supply of Quintennium back to his father's village in Peru, and had practically begged Marcello to never lose faith in his journey.

The years in South America had been difficult for Marcello. A boy raised alone in Alaska was hardly able to connect with his peers, and it was a lonely time for Marcello, despite the many crushes the traveling girls developed on the handsome boy. He had done his duty, but Marcello realized that delivering the crate to Peru was not the end of the responsibility but actually the beginning. He had closed that chapter, but began a whole new one here in the cabin with Anne and Penny. Marcello honored the directions and dug a small hole in the ground next to his father. He looked up to see an arctic fox looking at him inquisitively. Marcello nodded to the fox, and the fox stared at Marcello.

In his mind, Marcello heard the fox reassuring him that yes, his perception was correct. Penny really was the first of a new species of human beings, one that Mother Earth was very pleased to have created. Penny was luminous, and would drink of her mother's breast milk, and taste the other food of the earth, but did not really require that form of nutrition. She was fed by light, most effectively by the sun, and the rivers of light that flowed beneath the earth's surface, the same energy lines that had shifted and activated the Quintennium. The fox asked Marcello to forgive himself for his moments of doubt, and told him instead to focus on hosting and holding space for the spiritual center that he and Anne were going to be building in the valley he lived in. Marcello nodded his thanks to the fox for confirming all that Marcello's father had explained to him long ago.

Marcello took his bundle, Penny's bundle, and buried it in the hard ground. When he stood, the fox was gone, but the northern lights were in full effect, despite the time of day. The colors waved back and forth across the sky, and Marcello could make out the faces of both his mother and his father in the waves of color. He smiled at them both, then went back inside the cabin to tend to his small family and prepare for the future.

# About the Author

Denene has been a lover of books, reading and learning since elementary school. She is a practicing shaman, with a background in Drama instruction, Massage Therapy, Angel Intuition and Bodytalk. Writing this book was a wonderful, alchemical process for Denene, magically tying together  much of what she has learned since "falling out of the ordinary" herself in 2001. Her curiosity about the true cause of disease, and her search for fulfillment and meaning in life led her to study Shamanism with Marv and Shanon Harwood, of the Kimmapii School of Shamanism. Denene loves to speak and teach about Shamanism, Peru, and Ayni, and she has a shamanic practice in Calgary.

Denene has three amazing kids, and her and her family are enthusiastic supporters of Kimmapii Kids, a Canadian Charity that hand delivers satchels of school supplies to financially challenged kids in the Sacred Valley of Peru. Getting to know the people of Peru, and working with the Q'ero shamans has been one of the highlights of her life. This is Denene's first book, though the inklings of another story have begun to pop up here and there.

Are you ready to Fall Out of the Ordinary and Find Passion and Purpose?!

Go to www.dancewithfire.com to learn about "Dance With Fire" workshops and presentations.

**Ayni/Reciprocity Page**

Some of the shamanic concepts in this book were made available to me through the teachings of the Q'ero elders in Peru. I would like to reciprocate for that wisdom by donatiing 5% of all author profits from book sales to Kimmapii Kids, a Canadian charity that hand delivers satchels of school supplies to children in the Sacred Valley of Peru. Help us educate the world!
www.kimmapiikids.org

Cover Art Credit: Nicholas Jones
Author Photo Credit: Anne Flanagan

**Are you an Evolutionary Leader with a message
and interested in becoming an Author of Influence?**

Denene Derksen is a graduate of the InspireABook program and a member of the Inspired Authors Circle. If you want to get on the path to be a published author by Influence Publishing please go to **www.InspireABook.com**

For information on the Authors circle and other Authors of Influence please go to **www.InspiredAuthorsCircle.com**

**Influence Publishing**

More information on our other titles and how to submit your own proposal can be found at **www.InfluencePublishing.com**

CPSIA information can be obtained at www.ICGtesting.com
Printed in the USA
LVOW10s2301180913

353058LV00001B/7/P